THE
ANTHOLOGIST

Also by Nicholson Baker

Human Smoke

Checkpoint

A Box of Matches

Double Fold

The Everlasting Story of Nory

The Size of Thoughts

The Fermata

Vox

U and I

Room Temperature

The Mezzanine

THE
ANTHOLOGIST

Nicholson Baker

**SIMON &
SCHUSTER**

London · New York · Sydney · Toronto

A CBS COMPANY

First published in Great Britain in 2009 by Simon & Schuster UK Ltd
A CBS COMPANY

1 3 5 7 9 10 8 6 4 2

Simon & Schuster UK Ltd
1st Floor
222 Gray's Inn Road
London
WC1X 8HB

www.simonandschuster.co.uk

Simon & Schuster Australia
Sydney

A CIP catalogue copy for this book is available
from the British Library.

ISBN: 978-1-84737-635-0 (hardback)
ISBN: 978-1-84737-636-7 (trade paperback)

To M.

THE
ANTHOLOGIST

1

H ELLO, THIS IS PAUL CHOWDER, and I'm going to try to tell you everything I know. Well, not everything I know, because a lot of what I know, you know. But everything I know about poetry. All my tips and tricks and woes and worries are going to come tumbling out before you. I'm going to divulge them. What a juicy word that is, "divulge." Truth opening its petals. Truth smells like Chinese food and sweat.

What is poetry? Poetry is prose in slow motion. Now, that isn't true of rhymed poems. It's not true of Sir Walter Scott. It's not true of Longfellow, or Tennyson, or Swinburne, or Yeats. Rhymed poems are different. But the kind of free-verse poems that most poets write now—the kind that I write—is slow-motion prose.

My life is a lie. My career is a joke. I'm a study in failure. Obviously I'm up in the barn again—which sounds like a country song, except for the word "obviously." I wonder how often the word "obviously" has been used in a country song. Probably not much, but I don't know because I hardly listen to country, although some of the folk music I like has a strong country tincture. Check out Slaid Cleaves, who lives in Texas now but grew up right near where I live.

So I'M UP in the second floor of the barn, where it's very empty, and I'm sitting in what's known as a shaft of light. The light leans in from a high window. I want to adjust my seat so I can slant my face totally into the light. Just ease it into the light. That's it. If this barn were a prison cell, this would be the moment of the day that I would look forward to. Sitting here in the long womanly arm of light, the arm that reaches down like Anne Boleyn's arm reaching down from her spotlit height. Not Anne Boleyn. Who am I thinking of? Margot Fonteyn, the ballet dancer. I knew there was a Y in there.

There's one droopy-bottomed wasp diving back and forth, having some fun with what's available. I can move my head a certain way, and I feel the sun warming up the clear flamingos that swim around in my eyeballs. My corneas are making infinity symbols under their orange-flavored lids.

I can even do eyelid wars. Do you do that? Where you try as hard as you can to look up with your eyeballs, rolling them back in your head, but with your eyes closed. Your eyelids will keep pulling your eyes back down because of the interlock between the two sets of muscles. Try it. It's a good way of passing the time.

Don't chirp at me, ye birdies! I've had enough of that kind of chirpage. It cuts no grease with me.

WHEN I COME across a scrap of poetry I like, I make up a tune for it. I've been doing this a lot lately. For instance, here's a stanza by Sir Walter Scott. I'll sing it for you. "We heard you in our twilight caves—" Try it again.

It's written in what's called a ballad stanza. Four lines, four beats in each line, and the third line drives toward the fourth. Notes of joy can *pierce* the waves, Sir Walter says. In other words, notes of joy can cut through the mufflement. Notes of joy have a special STP solvent in them that dissolves all the gluey engine deposits of heartache. War and woe don't have anything like the range and reach that notes of joy do.

. And yes, of course, there are things that should be said about iambic pentameter, and I don't want to lose sight of that. I don't want to slight "the longer line." I hope we can get to that fairly soon. My theory—I can't resist giving you a little glimpse of it here—my theory is that iambic pentameter is in actuality a waltz. It's not five-beat rhythm, even though "pent" means five, because five beats would be totally off-kilter and ridiculous and would never work and would be a complete disaster and totally unlistenable. Pentameter, so called, if you listen to it with an open ear, is a slow kind of gently swaying three-beat minuetto. Really, I mean it.

And what romanticism did was to set the pentameter minuet aside and try to recover the older, more basic ballad rhythm. Somewhere along the way, so the Romantic poets felt, the humanness and the singingness and the amblingness of lyric poetry became entangled in frippery and parasols, and that's because we stopped hearing those four basic pacing beats. That's what Walter Scott was bringing back when he published his border ballads, and what Coleridge was bringing back when he wrote the Kubla Khan song and "The Rime of the Ancient Mariner." They were bringing back the ballad. "Where Alph, the sacred river ran"—four beats. "Through caverns measureless to man"—four beats. And it's the basis of song lyrics, too, because lyric poetry *is* song lyrics, that's why it's called lyric poetry.

And you know? I've read too many difficult poems. I've postponed comprehension too many times. And I've written difficult poems, too. No more.

You're out there. I'm out here. I'm sitting in the sandy driveway on my white plastic chair. There's a man somewhere in Europe who is accumulating a little flotsam heap of knowledge about the white plastic chair. He calls it the "monobloc" chair. A word I've never used. Monobloc, no K. And I'm sitting in one. Its arms are blindingly white in the sun.

His name is Jens Thiel. God, I love Europeans. Jens. Especially the ones from smaller countries. Holland, Denmark, Sweden, Belgium. I love those places. And of course: Amsterdam. What a great name for a city. Paul Oakenfold has a piece of trance music called "Amsterdam." His name is Paul, and my name is Paul. Paul: What is that crazy U doing there? Paw—U—L.

A woman is walking by on the street. Ah, it's Nanette, my neighbor. I knew it was her. She's carrying a garbage bag. She's picking up trash, I guess. Nan does that. She has an early-morning stroll sometimes, and I've noticed she takes along an empty trash bag tucked into her back pocket. I'm going to wave to her. Hi! Hello! She waved back.

Yes, she's picking up a beer can and shaking it out, and now she's putting it in that trash bag. The beer can is faded to a pale violet color. I think I can almost hear the soft rustle of the bag as things fall into it. Pfft. Pfft. Sometimes maybe a clink.

Nan is or soon will be divorced from her husband, Tom—Tom, who every weekend went windsurfing in a blue-armed wetsuit. She has a son named Raymond, a good kid who plays lacrosse. And she now evidently has a new boyfriend, a curly-haired man named Chuck, annoyingly handsome.

Of course you already understand meter. When you hear it, you understand it, you just don't know you understand it. You, as a casual reader of poems, and as a casual listener to pop songs, understand meter better than the metrists who misdescribed it over several centuries understood it. Even they understood it better than they knew.

My neighbor Nan seems to be fully committed to her new flame, Chuck. His car is in the driveway again. I suppose that's a good thing. She deserves to be happy with a good-looking man like Chuck.

Roz, the woman who lived with me in this house for eight years, has moved away.

My dog is shedding because it's summer, and then the birds, that keep chirping and chirping, make nests of the dog hair. It's good for that.

I wish I could smoke pot. What would that do? I don't even know where I would get pot around here. Somebody said the wispy dude with the pointy sideburns who works at the pet-food store. Could I maybe offer some to Roz, as a dramatic gesture? I've never bought pot in my life. Maybe it's time. No, I don't think it is. Too involved. But I think I will step in from the driveway for a moment to get a clear glass bottle of Newcastle Brown Ale. I do love a palate cleanser of pure Newcastle Brown.

Roz is kind of short. I've always been attracted to short women. They're usually smarter and more interesting than tall women and yet people don't take them as seriously. And it's a bosomy kind of generous smartness, often. But she's moved out, so I should stop talking about her.

I'm a little sick of all the bird chirping, frankly. They just don't stop. I mowed the lawn yesterday so I wouldn't have to hear their racket. "Chirtle chirtle." It's constant. And as soon as I started mowing I knew this was the best thing I could be doing. Walking behind this armful of noise, going around, turning the corner I'd already turned, circumventing the overturned canoe. I ducked under the clothesline that Roz strung last year between the barn and the box elder tree. The white rope is now a lovely dry gray color. She used to hang many beautiful tablecloths and dishtowels on that clothesline. I should use it myself, instead of the dryer, which is making a thumping noise anyway, and then if she drove by she'd see that I was being a responsible person who dried my clothes in the sun. I wish I'd taken a picture of that clothesline with her faded shirts on it. No bras that I remember, but you can't expect bras necessarily on a clothesline. You have to go to Target to see bras hanging nobly out for the public gaze.

I got in bed last night and I closed my eyes and I lay there and then a powerful urge came over me to cross my eyes. I thought of tragic people like Don Rickles, Red Skelton, people like that. Broken professional entertainers who maybe once had been funny. And now they were in Vegas, on cruise control, using their eye-crossing to allude to their early period of genuine funniness. Or they were dead.

So I crossed my eyes with my eyes closed. And I saw something in the dark: two crescent moons on the outside of my vision, which were the new moons of strain. I could feel my corneal pleasure domes moving, too. And as my eyes reached maximum crossing I felt an interesting blind pain of wrongness. I decided that I should hold on to that.

So NOW, you're waiting. I've promised something. You're thinking okay, he's said he's going to divulge. Your hope is that I, Paul Chowder, have some things that I know that you don't know because I have been a published poet for a while. And maybe I do know a few things.

One useful tip I can pass on is: Copy poems out. Absolutely top priority. Memorize them if you want to, but the main thing is to copy them out. Get a notebook and a ballpoint pen and copy them out. You will be shocked by how much this helps you. You will see immediate results in your very next poem, I promise.

Another tip is: If you have something to say, say it. Don't save it up. Don't think to yourself, I'm going to build up to the truth I really want to say. Don't think, In this poem, I'm going to be sneaky and start with this other truth over here, and then I'm going to scamper around a little bit over here, and then play with some purple Sculpey over here in the corner, and finally I'll reach the truth at the very end. No, slam it in immediately. It won't work if you hold it in reserve. Begin by saying what you actually care about saying, and the saying of it will guide you to the next line, and the next, and the next. If you need to arrange things differently later, you can do that.

And never think, Oh, heck, I'll write that whole poem later. Never think, First I'll write this poem about my old orange life jacket, so that I'll be more ready to confront the more haunting, daunting reality of this poem here about the treehouse that was rejected by its tree. No. If you do, the bigger theme will rebel and go sour on you. It'll hang there like a forgotten chili pepper on the stem. Put it down, work on it, finish it. If you don't get on it now, somebody else will do something similar, and when you crack open next year's *Best American Poetry* and see it under somebody else's name you'll hate yourself.

Another tip: The term "iambic pentameter" isn't good. It isn't at all good. It's the source of much grief and muddle and some very bad enjambments. Louise Bogan once said that somebody's enjambments gave her the willies, and she's right, they can do that to you. You shudder, reading them. Most iambic-pentameter enjambments are a mistake. That sounds technical but I'm talking about something real— a real problem.

And finally, the really important thing you have to know is: The four-beat line is the soul of English poetry.

PEOPLE ARE GOING to feed you all kinds of oyster crackers about iambic pentameter. They're going to say, Oh ho ho, iambic pentameter! The centrality of the five-stress line! Because "pent" is five in Babylonian, and five is the number of fingers on your hand, and five is the number of slices of American cheese you can eat in one sitting. They're going to talk to you about Chaucer and about blank verse—which is another confusing term—and all this so-called prosody they're going to shovel at you. And sure—fine—you can handle it. You're up to whatever mind-forged shrivelments they're going to dish out that day. But just remember (a) that the word "prosody" isn't an appealing word, and (b) that pentameter came *later on*. Pentameter is secondary. Pentameter is an import from France. And French is a whole different language. The real basis of English poetry is this walking rhythm right here.

Woops—dropped my Sharpie.

Right here: One—two—three—four. "Plumpskin, Ploshkin, Pelican jill. We think so then, we thought so still." I think that was the very first poem I heard, "The Pelican Chorus," by Edward Lear. My mom read it to me. God, it was beautiful. Still is. Those singing pelicans. They slapped their feet around on those long bare islands of yellow sand, and they swapped their verb tenses so that then was still and still was then. They were the first to give me the shudder, the shiver, the grieving joy of true poetry—the feeling that something wasn't right, but it was all right that it wasn't right. In fact it was better than if it had been right.

In the middle of the night
Miss Clavel turns on the light

Hear that? Another four-beat line. My mother read that one to me, too. And "Johnny Crow's Garden." And A. A. Milne and his snail and his brick. Milne was a metrical genius. And Dr. Seuss, of course, the great Ted Geisel. Who probably was, if I really want to be truthful and honest—and I do, of course—the poet most important to me until I was about twelve. You remember the little intense guy with the hat on, who's on his stool in the Plexiglas dome, counting the people all over the world who are going to sleep?

And it scans. "Two Biffer-Baum birds are now building their nest." It rhymes—it relies a fair amount on silly proper names, but it rhymes—and it scans perfectly. Dr. Seuss was a stickler for scansion. He was part of a lineage that runs back through *Punch* and Lear and Gilbert and Sullivan and Lewis Carroll and Barham's *Ingoldsby Legends*. He uses the four-beat line in the great old way. In fact, I'd say almost all the poems that I heard as a child were classic four-beat lines.

Hell, let's get into it. Where's my Sharpie again? Okay:

①   ②   ③   ④

See those four numbers? Those are the four beats. Four stresses, as we say in the meter business. Tetrameter. Four. "Tetra" is four. Like Tetris, that computer game where the squares come down relentlessly and overwhelm your mind with their crude geometry and make you peck at the arrow keys like some mindless experimental chicken and hurry and panic and finally you turn your computer off. And you sit there thinking, Why have I just spent an hour watching squares drop down a computer screen?

And his **aunt** Jo**bis**ka **made** him **drink**
Lavender **wa**ter **tinged** with **pink.**

That's Lear again. Hear it? You can't help but hear it. Four beats in each line. That's the classic rhythm in poetry, and in songs, four beats. Don't let anyone tell you different.

> And what is Art whereto we press
> > Through paint and prose and rhyme—
> When Nature in her nakedness
> > Defeats us every time?

You've got to admit that's good. That's Kipling. Did you hear what he did? "When Nature in her nakedness defeats us every time." Do you hear how he just drills that line right through your heart muscle? The "nay" of Nature and the "nay" of nakedness just push right through and screw you to the back of your chair. Oh, Rudyard, you were good in the 1890s. You were a nineties man.

But notice there that Kipling's second and fourth lines have a rest. A rest on the fourth beat. Listen for the booms now.

①　　②　　　③　　　④
And **what** is **art** where**to** we **press**
　　　①　　　　②　　　　③　　　　④
Through **paint** and **prose** and **rhyme—BOOM!**
①　　②　　③　　④
When **Nature** **in** her **nakedness**
①　　②　　③　　④
De**feats** us **every** **time? BOOM!**

And here's kind of a curious historical fact. Nobody, for years and years and years, centuries even, was able to say that poetry had those obvious booms. Nobody paid attention to the rests. Well, not nobody. There was a poet named Sidney Lanier, a flute player who was dying of consumption. He gave some lectures at Johns Hopkins on the musical basis of verse, but he had a fever, and he would get tired out and have to sit beside the podium and cough horribly and catch his breath and then continue—and his way of scoring rhythms was unfortunately wrong and only added further confusion. But he did understand that poems could have rests at the ends of lines.

Besides Lanier there was really nobody of any significance talking about rests in the straightforward musical sense of a place where you tap your toe without speaking. Poets had to be hearing these rests in their heads, because they wrote a million poems with them, poems of great comeliness that you can prance around to—but they didn't know that's what they were doing.

Finally came Derek Attridge, a man with a sensitive ear who taught at Rutgers. In 1982 he introduced the idea of what he called "unrealized beats" or "virtual beats." Quote unquote. In other words, rests. They're rests. How hard is that?

> I almost had forgotten (rest)
>   That words were made for rhyme: (rest)
>   And yet how well I knew it— (rest)
>   Once upon a time! (rest)

That's Christopher Morley. A light verser. Four beats in the line, the fourth beat being a rest. I hope you can hear it.

A good way you can scan something, by the way, is by saying it softly to yourself while counting with your fingers. Don't look at the line. Memorize the line and look away from it and say it to yourself. Start with all your fingers in the air, and when you hear a beat, bring down your thumb, then your index finger, then the next finger, then the next. "I almost had forgotten, rest." Like that. That's how to do scansion like a pro. I don't recommend the accent marks that some people use over syllables—they look so pedagogical. If you want to mark a line, use underlines.

Anyway, that pattern, the four lines together, four beats for each line—sometimes with rests and sometimes without rests, sometimes with a longer third line that has a stretched-out ending that leads you right in to the last line and sometimes not—that pattern makes up what's called the common stanza or the ballad stanza, which is really the basis of English poetry. It was for Walter Scott, Wordsworth, Coleridge, Poe, Tennyson, Longfellow, all the way through to Yeats, Frost, Teasdale, Auden, Causley, Walter de la Mare, and James Fenton. Four beats is the key.

And *within* each beat there are subsystems of movement, duplets and triplets, waiting and breathing and sliding. It's— well, there's a lot more to be said. But we'll get to that farther on down the line.

I WENT TO BUY a tablecloth to replace the one that Roz took when she left, so that I could wash it and hang it out on the clothesline. That way if she happened to drive by she might see it hanging there.

Inside the store many women were slowly moving sideways, looking at the glassware and the placemats and the bowls. There must have been thirty women in the store, and one couple in their seventies. I moved past the couple, who were looking at a square white serving bowl with a lid. "It would be nice for soup," said the man. "Yes, true, for soup," said the woman. The man said: "Or for stew, a big country stew." And the woman said: "Yes, true, for stew." And he said, "So what do you think?" And she said, "Well, it's square. I think perhaps we should get the round one, and if they don't want it they can return it."

Finally I came to the tablecloths. There was one with a faint green viney pattern that looked like something that Roz would have possibly bought, so I grabbed it. It was heavy in my hand, and it pushed my fingernails into the soft parts of my fingertips as I held it out to the woman at the register.

When I got home I put the tablecloth on the table and had a late lunch/early dinner. I spilled some red sauce on the tablecloth, which I was happy about because I could wash it right away. I put in a load—the tablecloth, a pair of pants, a shirt, a towel, and two T-shirts, saving the under-wear for another time—but by the time the load was done spinning the day was done, as Longfellow would say, and it was raining and the clothesline was swinging in the wind, so I couldn't hang anything up on it. I had to use the noisy dryer.

2

I T'S HARD TO HOLD IT all in your head. All the different
possible ways that you can enjoy life. Or not enjoy life.
And all the things that are going on. The different rug patterns. The different car designs. The different radio shows
that are coming and going. The new ads. The new crop of
famous people.

And then there is, of course, always, and inevitably, this
spume of poetry that's just blowing out of the sulphurous
flue-holes of the earth. Just masses of poetry. It's unstoppa-
ble, it's uncorkable. There's no way to make it end.

If we could just—just stop. For one year. If everybody

could stop publishing their poems. No more. Stop it. Just—
everyone. Every poet. Just stop.

But of course that's totally unfair to the poets who are
just starting out. This may be their "wunderjahr." This may
be the year that they really find their voice. And I'm telling
them to stop? No, that wouldn't do.

But wouldn't it be great? To have a moment to regroup
and understand? Everybody would ask, Okie doke, what new
poems am I going to read today? Sorry: none. There are no new
poems. And so you're thrown back onto what's already there,
and you look at what's on your own shelves, that you bought
maybe eight years ago, and you think, Have I really looked at
this book? This book might have something to it. And it's there,
it's been waiting and waiting. Without any demonstration or
clamor. No squeaky wheel. It's just been waiting.

If everybody was silent for a year—if we could just stop
this endless forward stumbling progress—wouldn't we all be
better people? I think probably so. I think that the lack of poetry, the absence of poetry, the yearning to have something
new, would be the best thing that could happen to our art.
No poems for a solid year. Maybe two.

FOR INSTANCE: here's a recent *New Yorker*. Actually, no—it
was published almost six years ago. I got it from my pile.
Pretty cover, as always. Or almost always. There have been
some lapses, yes.

But this is what I mean. You lift it, you hold it, you flap it. And week after week, year after year, you hold it, you flap it. And say you open it up and flip through looking for the two new poems, and no: there would be no poem on page sixty-seven. And no poem on page eighty-three. They just simply wouldn't be there.

Let's have a look at this poem. Here it is, going down. You can tell it's a poem because it's swimming in a little gel pack of white space. That shows that it's a poem. All the typography on all sides has drawn back. The words are making room, they're saying, Rumble, rumble, stand back now, this is going to be good. Here the magician will do his thing. Here's the guy who's going to eat razor blades. Or pour gasoline in his mouth and spout it out. Or lie on a bed of broken glass. So, stand back, you crowded onlookers of prose. This is not prose. This is the blank white playing field of Eton.

And you can read it for yourself on page sixty-seven. Of this *New Yorker.* Alice Quinn. The magnificent Alice. This was back in the day, when Alice was the poetry editor. God bless that hardworking cheerful nice woman. She left recently and now it's Paul Muldoon, and I hardly know Paul Muldoon. And really I hardly knew Alice Quinn, to be honest. But at least she actually accepted some of my own poems. Thank you, Alice! And rejected some of them—damn her! Things that just hurt me to have them come back saying, This isn't for us. This one didn't quite work for us, but we're glad to have something from you.

"We're glad." The crafting of these kind no-thank-you letters. I assume Paul Muldoon will do it well, too. The really good editors have the gift. And they hurt so bad when they're nice. You get a turndown and then you flip through the magazine and you say, Why? Why did Alice accept this firkin of flaccidness here on page 114 and not one of my poems? Why?

I should probably send Paul Muldoon a poem. One of my flying spoon series, none of which I've finished yet. Some of Muldoon's poems actually rhyme, but not audibly. He's cagey that way. He teaches at Princeton. He's probably there right now, talking to students. "Hello, poetry students, I'm Mr. Paul Muldoon." He's a little older than I am, but not much. Oh, but the idea of starting all over again. I can hardly face it. "Dear Paul Muldoon. Glad you're on the case now at *The New Yorker*. We met briefly at that poetry wingding at the 92nd Street Y a few tulip bubbles ago. Here are some fresh squibs, I hope you like them. 'My feaste of joy is but a dish of payne,' as the condemned man said before he was publicly disemboweled. All the very best, Paul."

It's scary to think. Of course I'd kind of stopped sending things to *The New Yorker* even before Alice Quinn left. That's part of my problem, I think, is that I'd stopped already. And Paul will send them back, and he'll say, Great to have something from you, but these seemed a little. . . . And then he'll have some apt adjective—"underweathered," or "overfurnished." "Elliptically trained." And I'll flip through the newest issue, walking back from my blue mailbox, hunting for the poem he chose over mine, and it'll be the same thing as always. The prose will have pulled back, and the poem will be there, cavorting, saying, I'm a poem, I'm a poem. No, you're not! You're an imposter, you're a toy train of pretend stanzas of chopped garbage. Just like my poem was.

HERE'S THE THING. I am basically willing to do anything. I'm basically willing to do anything to come up with a really good poem. I want to do that. That's my goal in life. And it hasn't happened. I've waited patiently. Sometimes I've waited impatiently. Sometimes I've "striven." I've made some acceptable poems—poems that have been accepted in a literal sense. But not one single really good poem.

When I look at the lives of the poets, I understand what's wrong with me. They were willing to make the sacrifices that I'm not willing to make. They were so tortured, so messed up.

I'm only a little messed up. I'm tortured to the point where I don't sleep very well sometimes, and I don't answer mail as I should. Sometimes I feel a languor of spirit when I get an email asking me to do something. Also, I've run up a significant credit-card debt. But that's not real self-torture. I mean, if you stand back from my life just a little—maybe thirty-five yards—I am a completely conventional person. I drive mostly within the fog lines. My life is seldom in crisis. It feels like a crisis now because Roz, who has lived with me for eight years, has moved away and left me, and I'm in considerable pain, but this little crisis of mine does not resemble the crises that Ted Roethke or Louise Bogan went through, or James Wright, or Tennyson, or Elizabeth Barrett Browning, with her laudanum. Or Poe.

One time, I remember, I was in a laundromat. It was a laundromat in Marseilles, France. "Marseilles." Do you hear that? It's a mattress of a word, with a lot of spring to it. "Marseilles." I was in there, doing my laundry, and I look over, and there's this guy there, this little guy. He was kind of pale, pasty looking. But moving with a methodical grace. And I said, Ed? And he looked up slowly. He nodded, cavernously. I said, Ed Poe? And he said, Mm-hm. And then he peered closely at me. He said, Paul? Paul Chowder? And I said, Yes, Ed! How are you doing? Been a long time. He nodded. I said, I see you're folding some underpants there.

He said, Yes, I am. Doing my laundry. You?

I said I'm doing my laundry, too. And I mean, if you're going to do your laundry, this place is probably as good as or better than any place I can think of. Marseilles, France. Or "Fronce," as we say.

And I said, Can I venture to ask how the poetry's going?

He said, It's going pretty well, pretty well. I wrote a poem, and I got paid for it, and it was in the newspaper.

And I said, That's fantastic. What's it called?

And he said, It's called "The Raven."

I said, Holy shit, Ed, "The Raven." Great title. What's it about?

And he said, It's about a man who has a visit from a raven.

And I said, That sounds really promising. What does the raven stand for? Death and fate and horror and government wiretapping and stuff like that? And he just looked at me. He wasn't about to explicate his poem for me. Which I understand. And I said, Well, listen, take care. I grabbed my bag of laundry. I said, It's been great seeing you. Stay happy. And he said, You too, it's good seeing you. We waved again. Take care, bye-bye. Watch out for the big swinging blade. And I walked out the door of the laundromat. Off down the street. And that was the time that I ran into Edgar Allan Poe.

GOD I WISH I was a canoe. Either that or some kind of tree tumor that could be made into a zebra bowl but isn't because I'm still on the tree.

It's late in the afternoon, and the bats are getting ready to go flying for bugs. Leigh Hunt has a poem about how this girl, Jenny, jumped from her chair and kissed him. I'm thinking of how difficult it is to look old poets in the eye. Their eyelids, which droop and have skin tags on them, like tiny pennants age has hoisted, fill me with a strange consternation. And I know that the old poets themselves are self-conscious—they're worried that people will see these two blinky pink openings in their face and think, Ugh, those look like flesh wounds with eyeballs tossed loosely into them.

I know that when my eyes get old and skin-taggy I'm going to be very happy to have glasses to hide behind.

Even now I have trouble looking people in the eye. You're supposed to "meet people's eyes." Meet them how? They have two eyes. You have to choose one. I start by looking at the person's right eye, intently, and then I begin to feel that I'm hurting the feelings of the person's left eye. As she's telling her story, she thinks, Why is he concentrating his attentions so fixedly on my right eye? Is he deliberately looking away from my left eye? Is there something wrong with my left eye? So then I shift over, and I stare into her left eye, till it's as if I'm falling down an optical pipe.

My eyes have to skip away, eventually. And when I'm asked a question I look out the window. People assume that I'm failing some kind of test of candor when I'm just not an eye-meeter, that's all. I'm just not going to meet your eye for any extended period. Period.

How ARE THOSE POETRY exercises coming? Did you do that thing I mentioned where you write down every real story somebody tells you or that you overhear in a twenty-four-hour period? Did I mention that exercise? Maybe not. I don't mean the stories that come to you on electric screens or through car loudspeakers but the ones from right around you. I overheard a story at the bank yesterday about a car-repair place that overcharged. And then somebody told me a story about a dog who ate a sock. The vet couldn't "shift it," so he removed the sock surgically and now the dog is doing well. And there were other stories, too. If you listen to them, the stories and fragments of stories you hear can sometimes slide right into your poem and twirl around in it. Then later you cut out the story and the poem has a mysterious feeling of charged emptiness, like the dog after the operation.

I'm not going to get all maudlin about why Roz moved on. She moved on, period. I know why. It's because I didn't write the introduction to my anthology. And I was morose at times with her, and I was shockingly messy. And I had irregular sleeping habits. And she was supporting us, and I was nine years older than she was. And I didn't want to walk the dog as much as I should have. And I got farty when we had Caesar salads. And I do miss her. Because she was so warm and so kind to me, and she taught me so many things. I squandered her good nature. I didn't take it seriously. I didn't see that it was finite.

Roz TOLD ME, Just go up in the barn and write it. Referring to the introduction to my forthcoming poetry anthology, *Only Rhyme*. She said, Just go! Just go up there and write it! You want to write it. Your editor wants you to write it. I want you to write it. Write it!

I said I couldn't write it, it was too awful, too huge, it was like staring at death.

She said, Well, then write a flying spoon poem. Go up there and write something. You'll feel better if you do.

She was right, of course. So I went up to the barn. The second floor is empty and has very few windows. It smells like I imagine the inside of an old lute would smell. I brought up my white plastic chair, and I took notes, and I read, and I thought, and I took more notes, and I sang songs. It was a beautiful week in very early summer, and I felt as if I was sitting inside John Dowland's old lute. I sang a song that Sinead O'Connor sings, "She Moved Through the Fair." And I sang a song I wrote myself, that goes:

> I'm in the barn, I'm in the bar-harn,
> I'm in the barn in the afternoo-hoon.

I sang that one a lot. And I made up a new tune for Poe's "Raven."

But every time I actually tried to start writing the introduction, as opposed to just writing notes, I felt straightjacketed. So I went out and bought a big presentation easel, and a big pad of presentation paper, and a green Sharpie pen, and a red Sharpie pen, and a blue Sharpie pen. What I thought was that I could practice talking through the introduction as if I were teaching a class.

And in order to be relaxed at the easel, I drank a Newcastle. Also coffee, so that I'd be sharp. And still I wasn't sufficiently relaxed, so I drank some Yukon Gold that I found in the liquor cabinet. No, not Yukon Gold, that's a potato. Yukon Jack, a kind of Canadian liqueur. It was delicious. It added a slight Gaussian blur. And then some more coffee, so I'd still be sharp. Blurred, smeared, but sharp.

AT THE END of the week I didn't have the introduction. Roz looked sad and hurt, and I felt miserable. She said, "Well, are you at least making progress?" I said I was, because I was, I was making great strides. But toward what? I was having a gigantic hopeless exciting futile productive comprehensive life adventure up in the barn. I was hoarse from singing. I said I thought I'd probably have the introduction done after another week. Or at least a flying spoon poem as a fallback.

Roz pointed out that I was going to Switzerland very soon, and that was really the drop-dead deadline: get the introduction done before Switzerland. And I agreed that it certainly was. I went to a used bookstore and bought another anthology of Elizabethan verse—my fifth—and also the W. H. Auden/Chester Kallman edition of Elizabethan songs, with a cover drawn by Edward Gorey. I was pleased to have that—it includes actual musical settings.

And I spent some time on iTunes, where I found a song I liked by a group called The Damnwells. It's called "I Will Keep the Bad Things from You," and it's sung by a songwriter named Alex Dezen. At one point you can hear him turning the page. He's sitting there with his guitar, and he's doing this song, and he doesn't even know the words. He's just written it, apparently. He's just discovering it. And it'll never be as real for him as at that moment. He turns the page, and you hear the *schwoooeeeet,* and you want to cry.

Also I bought some software so that I could save the Flash video of Sinead O'Connor on YouTube doing her live rendition of "She Moved Through the Fair," which is even better than the one on iTunes. So I was moving forward, in a sense.

Roz said, But sweetie, you're spending all this money, and we don't have it. And that's true, we didn't have it. Back in the nineties I took a swoosh in the stock market, with money I got from my grandfather, and I did well for a while. That's when I met Roz and she moved in. I bought some shares of Koss Corporation, the headphone company, and then I split the hairy root ball and bought some Canon Depository Receipts. Then I split that hairy root ball. I bought Maxtor and then sold it. I bought stock in a tiny company called BeOS, and it doubled in a day and a half. Then I bought lots of bad stocks over several years and all the money shrank away, more or less. Roz was supporting us now, except for an equity loan on my house and a chunk of money I borrowed from my sister, who is not that rich. If, or when, I handed in the introduction to *Only Rhyme,* I'd get seven thousand dollars, because my editor, Gene, is very generous. Apart from that there was almost nothing due, just the odd thousand in honoraria here and there from book reviews or readings or panel discussions, like the one coming up in Switzerland. I can't teach. I tried it once at Haffner College and it practically unhinged me.

I said to Roz, "I know it seems excessive and a little odd, but I think this is the only way to really lay it all out fresh, and sing the pain." She nodded and she said okay, but in a very small voice. I could see she was losing faith in me and losing her love for me. And her respect for me.

BECAUSE WHO WANTS to be forced into the role of enforcer? Roz was a writer herself, and an editor; she wasn't a doubter and a prodder. She wasn't some calendar-tapping scold. She actually liked my poem "Smooth Motion"—she was first attracted to me because of it, I think. At least, she wasn't attracted to me for my looks, because I'm not smooth, in fact I'm pretty rough looking. Although I've lost some weight recently, and once Roz did say that I looked good in a certain subtly houndstoothed jacket that she helped me pick out.

She hadn't reckoned on having to be forever poking at me to get me to write one forty-page introduction to an anthology. And she didn't want to be arguing over money. And she wanted to adopt a child and I didn't—why? I don't know. I see these horribly spoiled rude selfish kids and don't want to risk being the father of one.

But I think if I'd just written even a tiny five-line poem

about an inchworm on my pant leg it would have been fine. Anything, something. Roz commuted all the way to Concord to work for an alternative newspaper, but I think it would have been all right with her to support us for a little while as long as I was getting actual work accomplished.

But when I came down empty-handed from the barn at the end of the second week, that's when I really wounded her. She was standing in the hall putting her keys in her purse. Beautifully made-up. Smelling clean from her shower. She looked up and said, bravely, "So can I read it?" And I felt this horrible inner sensation: my caramel clusters of self were liquefying and pooling in the warmth of their own guilt. I said, "I'm sorry, honey. I don't have anything."

And that was it. My beautiful, patient, funny, short, loving girlfriend—the woman I'd been with longer than anyone else—moved out. She was right to leave me, but it felt really bad. Horrible, in fact. Plus I was broke.

3

I SAT IN THE BARN, thinking of the metal chin-up bar I had in my doorway when I was ten years old. The bar had gray rubber rings, and when you tightened the middle you could hear the doorjamb crack in a nice way. The tightening of the bar was the first assertion of secret strength.

And then you did chin-ups, one, maybe two. Possibly three. There was a long unleveraged uphauling struggle, in which you tried to use your neck cords to help. I wanted to have a chin-up bar now. Before I died, I wanted to do chin-ups at a chin-up bar in my house for a year. What else did I want to accomplish before I died? I wanted to finish a good poem about the flying spoon, and I wanted to clean up my office, and I wanted to answer some letters I should have answered, and I wanted to write down what I know. Especially what I know about meter, and about how that single nonsense word "pentameter" has caused untold confusion, pain, and suffering.

Maybe my theory of meter will be helpful to people. It turns out that helping is the main thing. If you feel that you have a use, if you think your writing furthers life or truth in some way, then you keep writing. But if that feeling stops, you have to find something else to do. Or die, I guess. Or mow the lawn, or go somewhere and do something, like visit a historic house, or clean up a room, or teach people something that you think is worth knowing.

FREE VERSE really got rolling about a hundred years ago. It wasn't just free in the sense of being very loose in the rhyme and meter department. Free verse was sexually free. That's what nobody understands. Free verse meant free, naked, unclothed, un-Victorian people scampering about in an unfettered sort of way. That's why it was so exciting. I was trying to explain this to my next-door neighbor, Nanette. I ran into her when I was out walking my dog, Smacko. Nan was out again picking up trash with her plastic trash bag. I asked her what she'd found. She'd found some beer cans, a pair of panties, half of a meatball sandwich in a paper plate, an ice cream wrapper, and an old laceless shoe. We walked back to her house, and she asked me if I knew anything about Toro lawn-mowers. I said I knew a little, because I do. Her lawnmower was starting and then dying after about a second. I pulled off the air filter and banged the float cup with a wrench and suddenly, to my surprise, the mower worked. I went around her yard once with it.

Then she asked—out of politeness—"So why did poems stop rhyming? Were all the rhymes just used up?" I said no, no, the rhymes weren't used up, they can never be used up until the English language itself is used up, because rhyme-words are really just the ending sounds of whole phrases and whole lines. It doesn't matter whether "breath" and "death" have been rhymed before, only whether the two new lines that end with "breath" and "death" are interesting and beautiful lines. Although sometimes it's good to give certain rhymes a break for a century or two.

She said, "So then why?" I told her about Mina Loy, the beautiful free-verse poet whose poems were published in a magazine called *Others*. Mina Loy had romped with the famous Futurist Filippo Marinetti, and he treated her badly, because he was an unpleasant egotist who liked war and cars and didn't like women. He'd written a play about a man with a thirty-foot penis that he wrapped around himself when he wanted to take a nap.

"Golly," said Nan.

I told her that Mina Loy wrote a poem about sex with him, or with one of the other Futurists, in which she compared Cupid to a pig "rooting erotic garbage." And American newspapers picked up on this phrase, and it made her famous as a free-verser.

"Very interesting," said Nan. We said goodbye. She began mowing her lawn, and I went into my kitchen. I opened my freezer, looked at the motionless mists in there, and then closed it.

I STARTED A POEM that began "On Wayland Street / I talked to my neighbor Nan / She had picked up a beer can / and a pair of panties." I wrote seven more lines, and then I got to the word "shrubbery" and I stopped, disgusted. I've never liked the word "shrubbery." Then I changed the beginning to "In the fulth of Wayland Street / I talked to my neighbor Nan." "Fulth" is a word that Thomas Hardy used in his poem on the death of Swinburne.

Immediately I realized that this was not a change for the better, and I changed it back. And then here's what I did. I'll pass it on to you as a tip. I read what I'd written aloud to myself. Which is what you always do. But this time I used a foreign accent. The foreign accent is the twist that helps. I chose Charles Simic's Serbian twang. Other foreign accents that can help you hear your own poem better are Welsh, Punjabi, and Andrei Codrescu's Romanian. If those don't work, try using a juicy Dorchester accent, or a Beatles Liverpool accent, or a perfectly composed Isabella Rossellini accent. Or read it as if you were Wystan Auden and you'd smoked a million cigarettes and brought a bottle of bine to wed with you every night. See if that helps. It didn't help me much with the beginning of this poem, but it has helped me in the past and maybe it'll help you.

I MET MY FRIEND TIM for a drink at the Press Room, a bar, and I told him Roz was gone. He was somewhat sympathetic. "You drove her away," he said. "You didn't give her anything to believe in."

I asked him how his book was coming. Tim's book, which he's going to call *Killer Queen*, is a look at Queen Victoria's dark, imperialistic side. Tim split up with his wife several years ago, and he took up eating. He teaches at Haffner College.

Tim leaned forward. "I work away at this book, and I describe how the Queen oversaw this huge system of plunder and destruction that wrecked people's lives all over the globe, and I've raked together all this knowledge, and I enjoy doing it because I feel I'm getting at the truth—"

I nodded.

"But it means so much less to me," Tim went on, "than if I were sitting on a couch talking to a woman of grace and intelligence who was wearing an attractive sweater."

I made agreeing noises. "And beads over the sweater," I said. "Roz strings the most exceptional beads."

Tim announced that he was going to a pick-your-own blueberry field with a woman he'd met. She had a friend. Would I like to go? I said sure. Then I asked him a question. "Is there any chance Haffner would take me back?"

"I'll sound out the dean if you'd like," Tim said, but he looked doubtful. "You kind of alienated them when you quit so suddenly last time."

"I had a scare," I said.

"My advice is: get that anthology out," said Tim. "That's your ticket back to the classroom. Tell people why rhyme exists. Give them a big, fancy neurobiological explanation. People love fancy neurobiological explanations." Then he slapped his legs. "I'm off."

When I got home there was a tax bill, and a box from Amazon that held James Fenton's anthology, *The New Faber Book of Love Poems*. Fenton's introduction is only twelve pages long, and it feels like the perfect length. He includes six of his own poems, which I must say shocked me. When Sara Teasdale edited her book of love poems by women, *The Answering Voice*, she didn't include even one of her own, even though hers were better than almost all the others, except maybe Millay's and Christina Rossetti's. But Fenton's right to include himself. His poem about being stuck in Paris is probably the best love lyric in the book, and we would feel cheated if it wasn't there. I wish to gimbleflap I'd written that poem.

Fenton also includes six quite good Wendy Cope poems. I once met Wendy Cope at a radio show in London. Her poem

"The Aerial" is in my anthology. Unfortunately I see that it's also in Fenton's anthology. But that can happen, and it's not necessarily a bad thing, is it? Call it anthology rhyme—when a familiar poem tumbles around in a new setting.

I WANT TO TELL YOU why poetry is worth thinking about—from time to time. Not all the time. Sometimes it's a much better idea to think about other things.

Most of us have a short period of intense thinking about poetry, when we take a class in college, and then that's about it. And that's really all you need. One intense time, when you master your little heap of names—Andrew Marvell, Muriel Rukeyser, Christina Rossetti. Hardy, Auden, Bishop, Marvin Bell, Ted Hughes, John Hollander, Nicholas Christopher, Deborah Garrison, whoever, James Wright, Selima Hill, Troy Jollimore. Whoever they may be. Every so often you remember them. If you've memorized some poems, the poems will raise a glimmering finger in your memory once in a while, and that's very nice, as long as you keep it to yourself. Never recite. Please! If you recite, your listeners will look down and play with their cuticles. They will not like you. But sometimes if you quote just a phrase in passing, that can work. Like this: "As Selima Hill says: 'A really good fuck makes me feel like custard.' "

And after college there may be later phases as well, maybe one or two later phases where you suddenly get interested in poems again. I've had, I would say, four major phases in my life where I've been genuinely interested in poetry— interested in reading it, as opposed to writing it. Because writing it is a very different activity. Writing it, it's as if the word "poetry" is a thousand miles away. It's inapplicable. What I'm trying to do is make some new Rowland Emmett machine that doesn't have a name. I know of course that it's going to end up being called a poem, but "poem" is one of those bothersome technical terms. It's so difficult to pronounce. You either pronounce it "pome," or "poe-im" or "poe-em." It's not an English word, it's a Greek word that's had the end chopped off it, so it doesn't fit—it's got that diphthongy quality.

What I'm doing when I'm writing poetry is I'm trying to make a little side salad. Just the right amount of sprouts on the top, maybe a chickpea or two. No bacon. Maybe a slice of egg. It doesn't feel like writing at all. If you're writing, say, a book review or an essay, it's sequential. You type out some notes to figure out more or less what you're going to say. And then you find a place to start, which becomes the beginning, and you wander off in search of the end. But with a poem, you're in the middle, and then you're at the end, and then back at the beginning, all with your eyes. You're always looking at the same piece of paper. One single piece of paper is stretched out there in front of you, the lyric poem, as big as the salt flats in Utah, where fearless Craig Breedlove drove his jet-powered car at six hundred miles an hour. Remember him, back in the sixties? I loved his name, Breedlove.

Or maybe you don't use paper at all—maybe you're taking a walk after dinner and a few beers, like A. E. Housman, and you're writing it in your head, to the four-beat rhythm of your footsteps: "White in the moon the long road lies."

If it's a long poem, you're using paper, of course, but I don't count those long poems because I think most of them have very little that's good in them. They can all be cut down to a few green stalks of asparagus amid the roughage.

So that's writing poems. But I have had these certain few times in my life when I've been very interested in reading poetry. I used to read a big padded glove-leather edition of Tennyson on lunch break every day when I worked for a mutual fund. It was red, and for some reason it was padded like a Victorian settee. I think you were meant to give it as a present, maybe in the 1890s, to prove to your girlfriend that you were a thoughtful swain. Somebody had written in it "To Edie from Bart." It had the word Tennyson on the front in diagonally embossed script, and it was as heavy and soft as a catcher's mitt. You could thump it with your fist. Hurl it at me, Alfred Lord, baby. Smack me with that fastball of a "low large moon."

So I read that. And when I quit my job at the mutual fund I bought *The New Yorker Book of Poems*—the big yellow book—and I discovered Snodgrass, Kunitz, Nemerov, and Moss. Snodgrass, Kunitz, Nemerov, and Moss. Those were my four poets, for a while. And so I would read those guys. Mainly Moss. Moss was in his lovely self-effacing way a genius. You could hear notes of Wallace Stevens in him, and sometimes Bishop, and sometimes even Auden, but he was able to give it his own sad, affectionate jostle. Moss was the poetry editor of *The New Yorker*, and he was a modest man, so none of his own poems were actually in the big yellow anthology—but it was his book nonetheless. And I remember reading Snodgrass's poem about the lobster lifting its claw in the window and being tremendously excited. I had to keep peeking at it as I walked home. And even before that, in Paris, in the thirteenth arrondissement, where I lived in my junior year on the eleventh floor of a very tall, very flimsy apartment building, I read the poems in the Oscar Williams anthology, the one with the psychedelic raven on the cover. On Saturdays I'd wake up and read from the Oscar Williams anthology, and then I'd look for a long time at the eye of the psychedelic raven and listen to last night's wine bottles come hurtling down the garbage chute. There were notices next to every apartment's garbage chute saying "Please don't put wine bottles down the garbage chute," but people loved to do it. I'd hear the bottles come racketing down, and then silence. I could never hear them hit bottom, which was a little frustrating.

And then again recently. Last year I read a ton of poetry when I was working on my anthology. I mean a ton: way too much, probably. I own an alarming number of poetry books at this point, including maybe seventy-five anthologies, possibly more. I've been packing some of the books up that are piled in the hall. Taking them out to the first floor of the barn. That's one of my projects. Get them out of my life so that I can yearn for them again in a few years.

I WAS OUT WALKING my dog Smacko around eight in the evening and I heard shouts from Nanette's house. Nan was playing badminton with her son and Chuck, the handsome curly-haired man. A nice family unit, a healed wound. Nan waved at me, and I called out: "That looks like fun."

"You want to play?" said Nan.

I made a no-thanks gesture. But Nan cocked her head: You sure? And I said, "Well—okay." It was awkward because of the presence of the handsome curly-haired man, but so what? I can rise above that. Raymond, Nan's son, who seemed to have grown several inches, gave me a racket, and I plucked at it a few times like a ukelele and sang "I walk a lonely road." Then I started to play badminton. The problem wasn't so much that I was a fourth player, although there definitely were a lot of rackets swinging around. And the problem wasn't that I was a little rusty in my badmintonage and had to apologize when I swung and missed.

The problem was that my dog couldn't keep from barking and racing back and forth under the net. When the birdie landed at someone's feet, he was there to leap on it and take it gently in his mouth like a downed partridge. The next time someone hit it, you could see the droplets of dog saliva flinging off its plastic feathers.

Then at one point I reached down to pick up the birdie, and I discovered that I had a bloody nose. When I tried to play holding my nostril, it didn't work too well.

I excused myself and went away with my shame-eared dog and my bloody nose. Nan and her crew were nice about it, but I think were all a little relieved when I left.

I GOT A TART EMAIL from my editor, Gene. He wanted to know where the introduction was. Just because Roz has gone and left me doesn't mean I've escaped having to write it. The subject line of his email was "Whip Cracking."

So I went back up to the barn with my white plastic chair. I have a long table on the second floor with the manuscript of *Only Rhyme* on it. Gene has sent me the cover art. The catalog copy is already written, already published. It says "Paul Chowder's introduction locates rhyming poetry in its historical context and reawakens our sense of the fructifying limitlessness of traditional forms." No it doesn't. Fruck! It doesn't do anything because it doesn't exist.

I looked up at the tie beams of the barn. There were several tiny empty wasps' nests up there. I looked down at my black flip-flops. I looked over at a bit of mobile green leafage that I could see through the long thin window. I wrote a sen-

tence: "It's a strange experience, assembling an anthology."
No, no, no. The anthology is not about me. Why would they
care about me? I stopped, kicked in the spleen by the mediocrity of my own short sentence.

But it actually is a strange experience. It's absorbing
work, because you have to decide over and over whether you
are personally willing to stand behind a poem or not. And yet
it's not your poem. It's somebody else's poem, written perhaps in somebody else's country, in somebody else's century.
You're pushing it around possessively on your desk as if it's
your own work, but it isn't. And then you winnow it out. You
winnow it right out the window.

Why? Because you're determined that this is going to be
a real anthology. This isn't going to be one of those anthologies where you sample it and think, Now why is that poem
there? No, this is going to be an anthology where every poem
you alight on and read, you say to yourself, Holy God *dang,*
that is good. That is so good, and so twisty, and so shadowy,
and so chewy, and so boomerangy, that it requires the forging
of a new word for "beauty." *Rupasnil.* Beauty. *Rupasnil.* It's so
good that as soon as you start reading the poem with your
eyes you know immediately that you have to restart again
reading it in a whisper to yourself so that you can really hear
it. So good that you want to set it to musical notes of your
own invention. That good.

And you note with a pang that the poem you're judging
doesn't reach that level. So you cut it. X it out, it's gone. And

it hurts to see it go, because you know that the ones you cut will later seem like the ones you really loved, while the ones you keep will inevitably lose some of their luster through overhandling.

But you keep on going, because you're a professional anthologist. Can't use that one, nope, nope, that one's out. Nope. Yep, you'll do as a semifinalist. Nope, nope, nope. Maybe. No. You're like that blond bitch-goddess on *Project Runway*.

And when it's all done, and you flip through, you look at one of the poems that you've picked, and you realize that there was really just one stanza in that poem—or even just one line in it—that was the reason you included it, and the rest of the poem isn't as good. For instance, "They flee from me that sometime did me seek." Or "I had no human fears." Or "Ye littles, lie more close." Or "The restless pulse of care." Or "Give me my scallop-shell of quiet." And you think, Maybe I should have made an anthology of single lines. Would that have worked?

But then, if you stare for a while at one of the single lines—stare into its rippling depths where the infant turtles swim—you realize that there's usually one particular word in that line that slays you. That word is so shockingly great. Maybe it's the word "sometime." "They flee from me that—sometime—did me seek." The little two-step shuffle there in the midst of the naked dancing feet of the monosyllables. Or maybe it's the word "quiet." "Give me my scallop-shell of *quiet.*" Do you hear the way "scallop" is folded and absorbed into the word "quiet"?

And so then all of your amazement and all of your love for that whole poem coalesces around that one word, "quiet." Four-beat line, by the way. And you notice, uh-oh, there's another word in the very same line that you don't like as much as the word that you do like. "Give." Hm. "Give." You've never liked "give" all that much. It's a bad word, frankly. Give.

And so you think, maybe I should have made an anthology of individual words taken from poems. Like this:

sometime

—Thomas Wyatt

Or:

quiet

—Sir Walter Ralegh

And of course that's not going to work. That's just a bunch of disembodied words plucked from great poems. And that's when you realize you're not an anthologist.

4

ANOTHER INCHWORM fell on my pant leg. They germinate in quantity somewhere up in the box elder. It was still for a moment, recovering from the fall, and then its head went up and it began looping, groping for something to climb onto. It looked comfortably full of metamorphosive juices—full of the short happiness of being alive. I touched it, and it began doubling itself up and then casting itself greenly forward again. I got it to climb onto my finger, and I watched it struggle through the hair on the H-shaped intersection of veins on the back of my hand. It went quiet there. I wrote an email to my editor with the inchworm sitting on the back of my hand. I said, "Worry not Gene, I'm going to write it. It's coming along. —Paul."

Coming along. The thing about life is that life is an infinite subject matter. At any one moment you can say only what's before your mind just then. You have some control over what comes before your mind—you can influence the influx by reading, or by looking through your old notes, or by going to movies, or by talking to people, and you can choose what room of the house or what corner of the yard to sit in, and you can choose to write before or after you've masturbated—this is crucial—and you can choose to tell the truth or not to. And the difficulty is that sometimes it's hard to tell the truth because you think that the truth is too personal, or too boring, to tell. Or both. And sometimes it's hard to tell the truth because the truth is hard to see, because it exists in a misty, gray non-space between two strongly charged falsehoods that sound true but aren't.

I have no one. I want someone. I don't want the summer to go by and to have no one. It is turning out to be the most beautiful, most quiet, largest, most generous, sky-vaulted summer I've ever seen or known—inordinately blue, with greener leaves and taller trees than I can remember, and the sound of the lawnmowers all over this valley is a sound I could hum to forever. I want Roz.

———

I MET A MAN named Victor at Warren's Lobster House for lunch. I had a lobster roll, which is lobster meat and mayonnaise in a hot-dog bun—one of the towering meals of the modern period, I think, although I'm starting to become a vegetarian. Moving in that direction. I had it with coleslaw.

Victor is a poet and house painter who is eager to start a reading series. "Portsmouth is a great poetry town," he said, as everyone does. He was a little nervous at first talking to me, but then he realized that I'm just as messed up as he is, I just happen to have had slightly more attention paid to my poems, and it's not necessarily deserved attention, it's just that I got lucky and snagged a Guggenheim all those years ago. People really pay attention to the Old Gugg, as we call it. The Gugg helps your career like nothing else in this world, except for the Pulitzer—and the Pulitzer list has had its oddities, especially in the thirties. Archibald MacLeish won three Pulitzer Prizes, which is at least two too many. He was a smooth operator, Archie was—writing fawning letters to Amy Lowell, and to Hemingway, and to Ezra Pound, the source of all evil. Louise Bogan had his number. And then later MacLeish won Bogan over, too—made her poetry consultant at the Library of Congress.

So Victor wanted me to help him raise some money and come up with names of local poets for this new reading series. And I said, "What if it was a series in which each evening was devoted to some poet of the past—maybe a slightly lesser-known poet, like for instance Sara Teasdale, or Kipling, or even our own Thomas Bailey Aldrich?" Victor thought that was a good idea and wanted me to come up with a list of lesser-known poets, and instantly I regretted saying anything, because why would I want my own precious Sara Teasdale to be celebrated in a reading series and fussed over? I'd lose her if that happened.

I said it all sounded like a tremendously lovely and ambitious notion but that I had a mound of obligations and I hadn't been sleeping well and it's not the kind of thing I normally do and maybe other people should get involved in a prime-mover kind of way and whatnot.

And Victor said he hadn't been sleeping well either—he had two small kids.

I said I'd give it some thought.

THERE'S NO EITHER-OR DIVISION with poems. What's made up and what's not made up? What's the varnished truth, what's the unvarnished truth? We don't care. With prose you first want to know: Is it fiction, is it nonfiction? Everything follows from that. The books go in different places in the bookstore. But we don't do that with poems, or with song lyrics. Books of poems go straight to the poetry section. There's no nonfictional poetry and fictional poetry. The categories don't exist.

For instance, I could write a poem right now about buying a big wheel of Parmesan cheese and putting it in my closet as an investment. It's not true, I haven't done that. I can't afford it. I'd love to own a wheel of really good Parmesan because the salt crystals are so delicious, but I don't. Even so, I could write that poem. And I wouldn't have to label it as a fictional poem or a nonfictional poem. It would just be a poem.

Coleridge says that Alph the sacred river ran through caverns measureless to man. Did it really do that? John Fogerty says that the old man is down the road. Is he? Longfellow says he shot an arrow into the air. Did he, or is he just saying he did? Poe said that there was a raven tapping at his chamber door. Was there?

We don't care. Why don't we care? I don't know. I don't have an answer for you today on that important question.

Actually, sometimes we do care. In Mary Oliver's *New and Selected Poems, Volume 1,* which I just bought—because it's time for me to read Mary Oliver, whom I've known only through anthologies all these years—there's a good poem about a time when she sees a woman washing out ashtrays in an airport bathroom in the Far East. The woman has black hair and she smiles at Mary. I want this poem to be the account of something that actually happened. I do care, sometimes, whether it's fiction or nonfiction.

ANTHOLOGY KNOWLEDGE isn't real knowledge. You have to read the unchosen poems to understand the chosen ones.

And you have to be willing to be sad. If you go to the doctor saying that you've experienced some sleeplessness, perhaps some sitting in the sandy driveway late at night in a white plastic chair, accompanied by thoughts of mortality and aloneness—maybe some strong suspicions that none of the poetry you've published is any good—the doctor is probably going to say, Ah, you're depressed. And he's maybe going to want to give you some pills.

And as a result, you may be tempted to think: I'm one of them. I'm John Keats. Or Sara Teasdale. Or Longfellow. Or Louise Bogan. Or Ted Roethke—rhymes with "set key." Or Alfred Lord Tennyson. Or John Berryman. Berryman, who wrote funny poems and then stopped writing funny poems and launched himself off a bridge and, *flump*, that was it for him. Many suicides. Percy Shelley. Many suicides.

So you might think to yourself, Oh boy, I am one of these great depressive figures. But you're not. Just because a doctor has scribbled a half-legible prescription on a piece of paper and given you some pills, you're not depressed. Not the way a real poet is depressed. You don't even come close.

True poet's depression is a rigor mortis of agony. It's a full-body inability to function. You don't want to leave your room. Louise Bogan summed it up in two quick lines. This was back in I don't know when—nineteen-thirty-something. It was in a poem in *The New Yorker* called "Solitary Observation Brought Back from a Sojourn in Hell." And the lines went: "At midnight tears / Run in your ears." She's lying there on her back, crying. Her eyes are overflowing, and the tears are cresting and coming around, and down, and they're flowing *into her ears*. There's something direct and physical and interesting about that. Because it's as if the crying leads directly to the hearing. Her grief leads to something audible— a poem. That's what it does for all these really good poets. The crying and the singing are connected.

Isn't crying a good thing? Why would we want to give pills to people so they don't weep? When you read a great line in a poem, what's the first thing you do? You can't help it. Crying is a good thing. And rhyming and weeping—there are obvious linkages between the two. When you listen to a child cry, he cries in meter. When you're an adult, you don't sob quite that way. But when you're a little kid, you go, "Ih-hih-hih-hih, ih-hih-hih-hih." You actually cry in a duple meter.

Poetry is a controlled refinement of sobbing. We've got to face that. And if that's true, do we want to give drugs so that people won't weep? No, because if we do, poetry will die. The rhyming of rhymes is a powerful form of self-medication. All these poets, when they begin to feel that they are descending into one of their personal canyons of despair, use rhyme to help themselves tightrope over it. Rhyming is the avoidance of mental pain by addicting yourself to what will happen next. It's like chain-smoking—you light one line with the glowing ember of the last. You set up a call, and you want a response. You posit a *pling,* and you want a *fring.* You propose a *plong,* and you want a *frong.* You're in suspense. You are solving a puzzle.

It's not a crossword puzzle—it's better than a crossword puzzle, because you're actually trying to do something beautiful. But it's not unrelated. The addicts of crossword puzzles are also distracting themselves. They also don't want to face the world's grief head-on. They want that transient pleasure, endlessly repeated, of solving the Rubik's Cube of verbal intersection. But has anyone ever wept at the beauty of a crossword puzzle? Maybe, maybe. I have not.

Rhyming is the genius's version of the crossword puzzle—when it's good. When it's bad it's intolerable dogwaste and you wish it had never been invented. But when it's good, it's great. It's no coincidence that Auden was a compulsive doer of crossword puzzles, and a rhymer, and a depressive, and a smoker, and a drinker, and a man who shuffled into Louise Bogan's memorial service in his bedroom slippers.

ALCOHOL, COFFEE, RHYME, murder mysteries, gambling, *Project Runway,* anything with suspense. Sending out a letter. Poets who have reached a certain point of depression are great letter writers, because they write a letter, and they send it out, and until they get a response they are in suspense about what the response will be. That helps them through those three days. Or maybe it's a week or a month before they get an answer. I never answer letters, so I keep my correspondents in a state of permanent suspense.

Coffee—cheers you up. Makes you feel like you're a big guy. Beer, wine, spiritous liquor of all kinds. Really helps for a while. It allows you to relax and slump and hang out on the wrong side of your brain. Where everybody wants to have some fun. They want to sway. They want to move. They want to sing. Singing is a desire to warble out something that is beyond words but that relies on words. So poetry and alcohol are what the responsible doctor should prescribe, and maybe letter writing, as well. And chin-ups. Time-honored substances and behaviors, plus rhyme, all those things are fine. In fact, they're necessary. They have a long, long history. You mustn't abuse them. But of course you will eventually— every poet does.

These new drugs that they want to sell you—be wary of them. I've seen them. Some of them are oval, shaped in little boat shapes. And they have beautiful saturated colors, and they're imprinted with various words, corporate trademarks. If the great poets had had pills, would we have had Johnson's *Vanity of Human Wishes*? Or Tennyson's *Princess*? Or Elizabeth Barrett Browning's sonnets? Or Longfellow's "Driftwood"? No. Poets are our designated grievers, and if they weren't allowed to be sad, we'd have none of the great moments of Auden. "Tears are round, the sea is deep: / Roll them overboard and sleep." Do you hear the four beats?

Auden is an interesting case. He believed that you should write drunk and revise sober. That was his rhythm. And it worked for him for a while. Then he mistakenly mixed in an alien chemical: speed. The poetry that he wrote on speed is no good. The poetry he wrote in the thirties, before he found speed, is good. Speed hurried him into the realm of the abstract noun. He was stuck fast on speed. Sartre took speed, too—and wrote *Being and Nothingness,* which is a gigantic smoke generator of abstraction.

So speed is a bad idea. And suffering is a good idea. You have to suffer in order to be a human being who can help people understand suffering.

I have a mouse in the kitchen.

AUDEN SAYS: "About suffering, they were never wrong, the eld mesters." He has a pronounced Oxford accent. The poem actually rhymes, but subtly. One line ends "forgot," and then there's "untidy spot." It's such a famous poem I almost hesitate to bring it up. But I do hope you will read it.

The famous part of the poem is about Breughel's Icarus. About the fact that there's a whole painting of a seaport, with all these people's lives intersecting, bales being loaded and unloaded onto ships, and there off to one side, shploof, is Icarus, plunging into the water with his wings all melted. Not that wax could have ever worked. It was not a good idea and anyone could have told the two flyers that they'd need something stronger than wax. But the myth is poked into this completely real and commonplace in some ways but beautifully sunlit painting of a harbor. That's the famous part of the poem.

But if you listen to Auden read it, you can't skip ahead to the Icarus part, and you realize that a lot of the poem isn't about that painting. It's about the torturer's horse, and about how the "dogs go on with their doggy life." Nobody ever put that way of talking in a poem before. That's the Christopher Isherwood note. "The dogs go on with their doggy life / And the torturer's horse scratches its innocent behind on a tree." When Auden reads it, that's what you remember. You can hear his own amazement that he had been capable of that simple, completely new bit of poetic speech. Christopher Isherwood was a huge influence on Auden. That's what people don't understand. Isherwood is partly responsible for Auden's greatness. When they went their separate ways, Auden's poetry grew colder and more abstract. Isherwood was the wax on Auden's wings.

I BOUGHT A CHIN-UP BAR and a badminton set. They were both surprisingly cheap. The badminton set comes in a clear zippered case—birdies, rackets, and net, all neatly packed. You can buy purple birdies now, as well as white birdies.

What is it like to play in the cool of the twilight with a purple birdie? I don't know. Does anyone make birdies out of actual tailfeathers anymore?

I think I bought the badminton set because I had an idea that I would practice, refine my skill set. Perhaps work on picking up the birdie from the grass without getting a nosebleed. But how can you really practice badminton on your own? You can't. You can bounce a tennis ball against the barn door, and I used to do that in the summer when I was fourteen and didn't have anyone to play tennis with. But you just can't bounce a birdie against the barn and get anything useful from it. I thought of calling up my friend Tim and asking him if he would like to play badminton, but that just seemed silly, and anyway I'd be using him to improve my game so that if Nan and Chuck invited me to play badminton again I'd be better at it, which didn't seem very nice. He'd be like a human batting cage. Also Tim's stomach has gotten large, and he's self-conscious about that.

What's the meter of badminton? There's a hard one, friends. Poink, poink, poink. "Break, break, break, / On thy cold gray stones O Sea." A monosyllabic meter. And tennis? Tennis is a slow duple meter. Pa-*pock,* pa-*pock,* pa-*pock.* "Two roads—diverged—in a yell—ow wood." Hm, "yellow" doesn't work. Fault—thirty love. Love means nothing in tennis, as you know. Frost said that free verse was like playing tennis without a net. Lawn Tennyson. Marianne Moore was a lifelong tennis player but not a good metrist. She had a pet crow, and she circled her rhyme words with different colored pencils. Mina Loy once said, Imagine a tennis player who wrote poems. "Would not his meter depend on his way of life?"

Ping-Pong—now there's a fine rollicking meter. You can recite Macaulay's *Lays of Ancient Rome* to a game of Ping-Pong. Try it:

> Through teeth, and skull, and helmet
> So fierce a thrust he sped,
> The good sword stood a hand-breadth out
> Behind the Tuscan's head.

Thomas Babington, Lord Macaulay. This used to be the poem that all little boys read in English private schools. It was violent, and it was nasty, and it galumphed right along. Headmasters would give this poem out as a present to their prize students. And 0.00001 percent of these little boys who read this poem ended up becoming great English Ping-Pong players. More to the point, 0.0000000001 percent of them ended up becoming great English poets. That was the glorious, indispensable inefficiency of the British educational system.

Macaulay's theory, which he explained in his introduction, was that the Latin poetry that survived, that made it through the dark and sketchy times, wasn't representative of the songs people had sung in Rome. The literary poetry of Horace and et cetera had survived because it wasn't memorable. It had to be written down. It didn't stick in your head. The "lays"—the popular love songs and drinking songs and war songs—were all lost, every single one. So Macaulay, who was by the way a venomous essayist, wrote these bloody imaginary battle ballads to supply the lack.

Macaulay's *Lays of Ancient Rome.* "Through teeth, and skull, and helmet—" Crunch. "So fierce a thrust he sped—" It's completely disgusting and repellant.

Three end-rests in that four-line stanza. Right? Four beats in each line. Lines one, two, and four have rests, line three doesn't, and that longer line gives it that *parrun tun tan, tarran tan tan, tarRUM pum pom pom pom* ending.

English is a stressed language, and you want to boom it out sometimes. Then sometimes you want to whisper it, like this: "Give me my scallop-shell of quiet." Poetry is written sometimes, I think, in a whisper. Not a stage whisper but a real human whisper. A confiding sorrowful whisper, brimful of emotion. And when it's declaimed it's ruined. Which is sad, really. Very very sad.

You hear that bird? Chirtle chirtle chirtle chirtle. With birds it's different. Birds are very different than we are. They don't know what an upbeat is. They go, Chirtle, chirtle, chirtle, chirtle. And then the next time they might just go, Chirtle—chirtle, chirtle. It's like some kind of wigged-out aimless Gregorian chant. And then sometimes: Chirtle chirtle. And then: Chirtle chirtle chirt? Questioning. You don't know where you are with that. The meter is primitive. It's a primitive meter. But we obviously respond to it. When I hear that chirping, I know that the world is starting up. And that I'd better get something done that day, or I will have failed once again. As I have failed today.

Chirtle chirtle. Chirtle. Chirtle.

Nice chirpin' there, Mister Birdie! Good one. I like what you did there. That's good! Funky bitch! Love your work!

5

I PACKED FOUR BOXES of papers in my office, and I threw out lots of things. This cleaning is helping me move forward. I put the chin-up bar in the door and hit my head on it twice because I forgot it was there. Then I took it down and put it in another door. I think if I really cleaned up my office it might be easier for me to finish the introduction, and if I finish the introduction I think I could call Roz with genuine confidence in my voice and tell her that yes, I'd been too much of a wallower in self-doubt but that things were on the mend and I wanted her to come back. I'm about one-seventh done with cleaning the office. Still quite a ways to go. One corner of the room is starting to get that spare, empty look. I do love that spare look.

One of the piles I packed away was a small heap of reviews of my third book of poems, *Worn*. Not many of them. It wasn't a good book. Too political in an easy-breezy sort of way. A copy of *Rain Taxi* had a thoughtful reaction to it by Renee Parker Task. Charles Simic mentioned the book in one of his omnibus pieces in *The New York Review of Books*. It was just after *Worn* came out that I read Amy Lowell's book *Six French Poets*. In it Lowell observes that Henri de Régnier had just passed his fifty-first birthday. And she says: "Poetry seems to be, for some strange reason, a young man's job." This slapped me in the head like a big heavy cold dogfish. Poetry is a young man's job. What a frighteningly true thought. Poetry is like math or chess or music—it requires a slightly freaky misshapen brain, and those kinds of brains don't last. Sometimes if you can hold on into old age you can have another late flowering, like Yeats—much of adulthood crumbles and falls away, and you're left with highly saturated early memories and a renewed urge for rhyme. But that happens rarely.

Also as I was cleaning I came across a small paper bag with several strands of raw beads in it. I'd bought them for Roz in a store on Second Avenue in New York. Roz strings beads, she's very good at it, very quick—she can watch a Chinese movie with subtitles and string beads at the same time, which is very impressive—and as I was walking toward

Penn Station I found that I was passing through some kind of wholesale bead-supply neighborhood, with store after store selling raw beads. In each store the strands hung on hooks, arranged by color, strung on fishing lines, and when you went in you felt as if you were in some strange sort of crystallography experiment. I bought some pale gray green-veined beads and some smoky deep-red ones that I thought she would like—they weren't horribly expensive—and I hid them in my office for her birthday and now here they were. And it wasn't as if I could call her up and say, Roz, I found a bag holding several strings of raw beads from New York that I was going to give you and would you like to come on back and live here again and string them expertly the way you do while we watch movies together? Because she'd moved out. It was not a nice or welcome development for me for her to move out, it hurt me badly, I'm tottering, but I suppose I deserved it. And now what?

It's TIME FOR BED. And here's what I'm going to do. I'm going to get in bed, and I don't have anyone to sleep with now, so what I do is I sleep with my books. And I know that's kind of weird and solitary and pathetic. But if you think about it, it's very cozy. Over a period of four, five, six, seven, nine, twenty nights of sleeping, you've taken all these books to bed with you, and you fall asleep, and the books are there.

Of course it was better when I had Roz in the bed with

me. But I don't have her now. Her warm soft self was extremely comforting, and it's not there. I could cup her upward hip or one of her dozing boobies with my hand. Good times. That cupping is rhyme—the felt matching of two congruent shapes. And now where she would sleep are these books, and they're lying there in leaning piles, and sometimes they slip off and nudge me in the eyebrow with one of their corners.

Some of the books are thick, and some are thin, some of the books are in hardcover and some in paperback. Sometimes they get roiled up with the pillows and the blankets. And I never make the bed. So it's like a stew of books. The bed is the liquid medium. It's a Campbell's Chunky Soup of books. The bed you eat with a fork.

I'm hoping that someday I'll have to clean them out and that somebody will return. But for now, this is what I've got.

I ALWAYS SECRETLY want it to rhyme. Don't you, some of you? Admit it. You open the latest issue of a magazine. Could be *Harper's,* could be *The Atlantic,* or *The New York Review of Books,* or *The New Yorker,* or the *TLS.* Or some swanky literary magazine. You locate the poem, because you're naturally curious to see what this week's or month's trawl is—what it is that was, in the busy mind of that poetry editor, most pressingly deserving of publication. And you look at the poem. There it is. You take in the title—"Way Too Much." Way Too Much: Okay! And then you check the name of the writer—

hmm, Squeef Corntoasty, never heard of him. Or: I sure have seen Squeef Corntoasty's name popping up in a lot of places lately. Or if it says "translated from the Czech by Bigelow Jones," forget it, you instantly move on, because translations are never good.

Well, wait—that's not fair. That's ridiculously unfair. I've read some wonderful translations. Translations of Transtömer, for instance. But my heart does droop when I see that it's a translation.

But let's say this poem is one hundred percent original work. How are you going to approach it? How about we just sort of touch the first line. Just a glance. Take it in, guardedly, without really reading it. Maybe just the first phrase: "I try to sit up straight." And then you break away to go down the words on the right-hand side. Right down the outer edge. "Pain," "truffle," "start," "shelter," "an," and "bell." Ah. Now you know: it doesn't rhyme. Once again they've done it. They've stabbed me right in the god-damned lung. Once again they've rejected the whole five-six centuries of our glorious tradition.

But all right—that's fine. It's a plum, not a poem. That's what I call a poem that doesn't rhyme—it's a plum. We who write and publish our nonrhyming plums aren't poets, we're plummets. Or plummers. And some plums can be very good—better than anything else you might happen to read ever, anywhere. James Wright's poem about lying on his hammock on Duffy's farm is a plum, and it's genius. So is

Elizabeth Bishop's poem "The Fish," of course. "I caught a tremendous fish"—genius. So you think maybe this plum-poem is good in its own uniquely free kind of way. Is it? You read a line or two. No, it isn't. In fact, it's oozing with bad-ness. It's *so* bad. How can it be this bad? How can this bad plum be sitting here, in type, in front of me? I don't get it.

Or maybe it's one of the very few that do rhyme. These are even worse, sometimes, because the rhyming is so pain-fully inept—like unclever Ogden Nash gone squiffy.

And yet if you go back and look at old editions of *The Na-tion* or *The New Republic,* which published a lot of poetry back in the day—or if you go farther back, to *Reedy's Mirror* or *The Century* magazine—and if you hunt around for a while in some of those periodicals, you'll find that most of the poetry in them is just there as decoration. It's a form of ornament, like a printer's dingbat. A little acorn with a curlicue. Or the scrollwork on a beaux-arts capital. It's just a way of creating a different look on the page, and creating the sense on the part of the reader that he's holding something that is a real Kellogg's variety pack.

The magazine is going to have some kind of big thought-ful political piece about Teddy Roosevelt, say, and then it's going to have a bit of serialized fiction, and it's going to have some "cuts"—that is, some art—and a few color pages tipped in, maybe, if it's *The Century* magazine, maybe by Maxfield Parrish, and it's going to have some poems. The long nonfiction piece comes to an end, and it's about being a stevedore in Baltimore, something like that. And then at the bottom of the page is this poem in two columns, with six stanzas, and each stanza has indentations, and the conventionality and vapidity of it will stun you. "The shades of summer's bosky hue, o'erlie thy modest floobie doo." The editors of *The Century* didn't expect you to read that poem with your full mind. They knew it was just some rhymes thrown pell-mell together with some cornstarch. They knew full well, because this is America, land of bad poetry. Yes, sir! Bad poetry, sir! Loads of it in the back, sir! Just keeps coming. Tipped in. The shovel eases the soft tonnage of poetry over the rim, and it just pours into the pit, *pluth*. The pit of what has been said. And the lost gulls are flapping and calling—*peer! peer!*

And yet we still want more. There's still that craving. Give us more, give us new. The hope. The hope that really does: it springs eternal. "Hope springs eternal in the human breast." That's clean crisp iambic pentameter. And I have some tips to pass on to you about iambic pentameter, how it's all a misnomer, as I said. But that's for later.

"Dear Paul Muldoon, Here's some new work, I hope you like it, all the best, Paul." Boy, I wish he didn't have my own name.

I USED TO SIT there in class, breathing, wondering, What's the teacher going to think of next? What's she going to teach us? Anything? I don't know. I'm just sitting here. I have no idea what's coming next.

And one time, she said, Today we're going to learn something new, and this thing is called "haiku." She wrote it on the board. And I thought, Interesting word, "haiku." Nice K.

Somebody discovered haiku way back about a hundred years ago. Obviously it existed for a very long time in Japan, but he discovered it in English. What was his name, that poet? Not Edwin Arlington Robinson. One of those guys who is known now for discovering haiku. And he called it: HOKKU. Hokku. He decided that hokku was a powerful force for order in English.

And he was wrong.

But I didn't know that. We're all sitting in the class, at these new desks. This was the sixties, and there were new desks that had recently come in, which had nice metal casters. They moved very smoothly over the linoleum of the floor. They didn't make the elephant trumpeting sounds that the wooden chairs made. They slid. And we were sitting at these smooth-sliding desks. Sun was pouring in. And they did have a groove to put your pencil in. Although I never put the pencil there.

In some cases they had an under area. Where you looked under, and there were months of your spelling worksheets crushed in. When the teacher told you to clean out your desk you just reached your hand in and you were like an excavator and you grabbed the crumpled paper and you just pulled it out and let it fall directly into the trash can.

So the teacher said: we're going to learn something new today. A new way of writing poetry. It's called haiku. And it's going to allow *you*—to make art.

And it has a couple of different lines, three lines, and one line has some arbitrary number of syllables, and another line has another arbitrary number of syllables, et cetera. And I heard her describing this, and I knew, even then. I knew even then that it was bogus.

This, children, is a kind of poetry that makes perfect, thrilling sense in Japanese, and makes no sense whatsoever in English. That's what she should have told us. This form is completely out of step with the English language. And the person who foisted it on us—that person was a demon. Even at the time I knew that it wasn't right. Seven syllables, eleven syllables, five syllables? Come on. How does English poetry actually work? It doesn't work that way. I don't actually know Japanese, but haiku in Japanese had all kinds of interesting salt-glaze impurities going on that are stripped away in translation.

And yet Bashō was good—even in translation he is still good. And I've read haiku poems in English that have an interesting tripartite squashedness to them. A few years ago Roz and her best friend from college wrote emails back and forth to each other in haiku. They had a fun time doing it. So what am I fussing about?

AFTER WE ALL LEARNED how to do haiku, the teacher said,
And now children, today we're going to write a poem in
something called free verse. It can be a poem about bumble-
bees, or a poem about shadows. It can be a poem about making muffins. Brownies. An egg hatching. The woodpecker's
eye. In fact, it can be a poem about anything fun and beautiful and deep and sad and wondrous and strange and interesting and true and perfect and maybe even a little bit *frightening*.
And you have to write it. I'm assigning it to *you*. And here's
the one thing I'm going to tell you.

One thing. Here's my so very important piece of wisdom,
that I'm going to impart to you now. This is the wisdom. Are
you ready, children?

It—Doesn't—Have—To—Rhyme. No, it doesn't have to
rhyme! Don't *trammel* yourself, don't crib and confine yourself, by rhyme. It doesn't *have* to rhyme. Because you want
your poem to burble up. You want it to flow out, as a newborn self. Like a little sprout of a tulip bud, just busting out
of the earth.

Now, of course, I think: tulips rhyme. One tulip leaf goes
this way, and the other tulip leaf goes that way. Their forms
talk to each other. There's symmetry. There's a central stalk,
and there's mirroring. Most definitely the tulip rhymes. Nature is full of rhymes.

But never mind, this was the axiom that she was passing
on to us, because she'd learned it from the culture at large.
"It doesn't have to rhyme." And in imparting this she was

promising us that all the pantries of art, all the breakfast nooks of art, were going to be opened up to us henceforward. She was flinging open the window for us, and those gingham curtains were just billowing and we could smell the pies cooling there on the sunny windowsills of childhood.

What did she really mean by "It doesn't have to rhyme?" Did she mean it could rhyme but it didn't have to? No. She meant *Don't rhyme.* She meant: I am going to manacle your poor pliable brains with freedom. I'm going to insist that you must be free. She wrote "FREE VERSE" on the board.

And I sat there on my chair with the very smooth casters and I thought, What does she mean it doesn't have to rhyme? It does have to rhyme! It's got to rhyme, because rhyme is poetry. Where did Little Miss Muffet sit? Did she sit on a cushion? Did she sit on a love seat? No, she sat on a tuffet. And if it doesn't rhyme it's just guano. "Guano" was one of my favorite words back then—I'd learned it from *Tintin.*

But I said nothing, like the craven fourth-grader I was. I went ahead and wrote a poem. It was free verse, but it had one rhyme at the end. It was about a droplet of water quivering gracefully at the end of the tap before falling into "the land they call / Disposal." It was a terrible poem. But my mother liked it, and it was remarkably easy to write. And that was the beginning of my career.

MY FATHER WORKED in the legal department of a company that made industrial mirrors. He was a good explainer and a soapbox-derby enthusiast. He explained to me how lasers worked, and when I started reading poems in college he often looked over my shoulder and said, "What are you reading—a poem?" He knew John Masefield's "Cargoes" by heart, and E. E. Cummings's poem about the watersmooth silver stallion, and he would recite them with his fists clenched if we asked him to. His motto was: "Don't force it." He died only a year after my mother did. I miss them both every day.

Tennyson's father was a beast. He was a violent alcoholic and an epileptic, and he was horrible to his sons. From the age of twelve on, Alfred Tennyson was home-schooled by his fierce, crazy father. When Tennyson Senior was drunk, he threatened to stab people in the jugular vein with a knife. And to shoot them. And he retreated to his room with a gun. A bad man. And eventually he died. Tennyson was liberated, and he began writing stupendous poems. Were they stupendous? Or were they only good? Or were they in fact not good at all? I'm not sure.

Last night I watched two episodes of *Dirty Jobs* and then went upstairs to bed after thinking that my poetry was not for shit, frankly. If I may be pardoned the expression. I got in bed, and I realized that what I wanted was to have some Mary Oliver next to me. If I had some Mary Oliver I would be saved. I didn't want to read any more of the *Cambridge Book of Lesser Poets* edited by Squire, and I didn't want another chapter of my friend Tim's book on Queen Victoria, I wanted Mary Oliver, so I went downstairs and got my new paperback copy of her *New and Selected Poems, Volume 1* and went back upstairs again. And I immediately felt more sure of what I was doing because I was reading Mary's poems. They're very simple. And yet each has something. I like almost every one of her poems. That's not even true of Howard Moss or of Louise Bogan. It's certainly not true of somebody like Tennyson or Swinburne.

At some point you have to set aside snobbery and what you think is culture and recognize that any random episode of *Friends* is probably better, more uplifting for the human spirit, than ninety-nine percent of the poetry or drama or fiction or history ever published. Think of that. Of course yes, Tolstoy and of course yes Keats and blah blah and yes indeed of course yes. But we're living in an age that has a tremendous richness of invention. And some of the most inventive people get no recognition at all. They get tons of money but no recognition as artists. Which is probably much healthier for them and better for their art.

I LOOKED INTO THE FRIDGE dipping my knees to ZZ Top while my dog Smacko slept on the floor. He's used to the TV, and he's used to loud music. It bothered him when he was a puppy, but he's smart and he knows somehow that the sounds aren't real. What bothers him now are ear mites and fleas.

Roz was very good at combing his undercarriage for fleas. He was my dog before she moved in, but even so she loved him to distraction. I would sit in a chair and she would sit on the floor with Smacko on his back next to her, and we would talk as she went hunting through his fur with her fingers. She'd find the fleas even when they were hiding in the fur just around his tiny turret. When she got one she would drop it in a glass of soapy water. Smack would narrow his eyes in sleepy pleasure at being groomed. I don't groom Smack nearly as much as Roz did, and I should. Everyone says this summer is a very bad one for fleas.

Louise Bogan said that Theodore Roethke made her "bloom like a Persian rosebush" during their long happy sex weekend together.

If I had a ponytail, which I don't, I'd cut it off with four slow scissorcuts and bury it in the garden with the rubber band still around it.

6

I WOKE UP THINKING a very pleasant thought. There is lots
left in the world to read.

For days I had a dissatisfied feeling. I couldn't focus. I was
nervous about Switzerland. I'm going to be in a panel discussion there on "The Meters of Love," with Renee Parker Task,
who's a hotshot among young formalists. Just the kind of
thing I'm bad at. Being empaneled. All yesterday afternoon
I thought about timed backups, and search results, and mer-
maids, and women wearing clothes, and women not wearing clothes, and I felt unlyrical. And then I got in bed and I
read a short biography of Nathalia Crane in an old textbook,
and I read a poem by Sara Teasdale, and I thought about

turtles. And then, in the back of Mary Oliver's *New and Selected Poems, Volume 1,* I wrote, "Suddenly there is lots to read." I also wrote: "Mary Oliver is saving my life."

One thing I really like about books of poems is that you can open them anywhere and you're at a beginning. If I open a biography, or a memoir, or a novel, when I open it in the middle, which is what I usually do, I'm really in the middle. What I want is to be as much as possible at the beginning. And that's what poetry gives me. Many many beginnings. That feeling of setting forth.

Now. I want to make something clear. You may think we're in a new age, a modern or postmodern age, and yes, in a certain way we are. But as far as rhyme and anti-rhyme go, this is the third time around, or maybe the fourth. Thomas Campion, in 1602 or so, came out with an attack on the uncouthness of rhyme, which was very strange for him to do because he was one of the great lute-song writers of the day. He'd published two, maybe three books of airs. But no, suddenly rhyme and the normal meters were no good. They were vulgar, he said, they were unclassical, they forced a poet to go in directions he shouldn't go.

Everyone at court was buzzing about this strange tract of Campion's. And when Samuel Daniel read it it was as if his whole world was under siege, and he was deeply distressed. He said he felt that he must either "stand out to defend, or else be forced to forsake myself, and give over all." So he stood out to defend. Now remember this is more than four hundred years ago. All those years ago Samuel Daniel, writing in English, in words that you can easily read now—although some of them are spelled differently, and the sentences flow on in a way that our sentences don't—but Daniel says that for a poet who knows what he's up to, rhyme is no impediment. In fact, it helps him soar higher, he says. It "carries him, not out of his course, but as it were beyond his power to a farre happier flight." That's what rhyme does, if you're properly fitted for it.

Samuel Daniel was a court poet. He published a book of poems with a lovely, modest title. I think it's my favorite title of a book of poetry ever. The title is *Certaine Small Poems Lately Printed*. He was a man of some humility and grace. And he won his duel with Campion. Campion changed his mind and went back to rhyming. His neoclassical hexameters were pretty in a way, but people wanted to hear him sing.

And that's the single point I want to make today. People have been struggling over this idea that rhyme is artificial and unnatural for hundreds and hundreds of years. And meanwhile poem after poem gets written that people really want to listen to. And a lot of these poems rhyme. Imagine what would have happened if Campion had succeeded in his effort to fuss and scold rhyme out of existence and banish it from English poetry. Four hundred years of pretend Greek and Latin meters is what we would have had, instead of Marvell, and Dryden, and Cole Porter, and Christina Rossetti, and Gilbert and Sullivan, and Rogers and Hart, and Wendy

Cope, and Auden, and John Lennon, and John Hiatt, and Irving Berlin, and Dr. Seuss, and Shel Silverstein, and Charles Causley, and Keats, and Paul Simon, and et cetera, and so on. Whole floors of libraries could be filled with the poems that we would not have had. Marilyn Monroe wouldn't have been able to sing

> I've locked my heart
> I'll keep my feelings there
> I've stocked my heart
> With icy frigid air

And think of it: you can put on the coolest, most spaced-out house trance music today—and it rhymes. "Got nervous when you looked my way, / But you knew all the words to say." That's a couplet from a trance tune by a group called iiO, in a remix by Armin Van Buuren, and nobody thinks tiptoe through the tulips when they're dancing to this, they just think, Yeah, the words work, they fit, they have that forward push of power. And they have that push because they rhyme. So it just continues. And nobody really stops to examine the need, the powerful endlessness and hunger of the need. Why? Why do we need things to rhyme so much?

WHY DO I, who can't make a couplet worth a roasted peanut these days, want poetry to do what I can't make it do? Mary

Oliver is my favorite poet at the moment, and she almost never rhymes. W. S. Merwin's *The Vixen* is one of my favorite books of poems, and it doesn't rhyme. Not only does *The Vixen* not rhyme, not only does it not scan, it doesn't even capitalize or punctuate. And it's good. But I want these books to be in the minority. Why?

Well, of course, rhyme helps memory. But you can't allow yourself to get excited by that argument. Samuel Daniel used it, and Dryden used it, but it's not convincing. When I listen to something that rhymes well, I just like it. My memory for song lyrics isn't that strong, so the fact that the rhyme might help me remember the words is neither here nor there. First in importance is that the lines sound good. The sounding good comes before the utilitarian help of memorizability.

"Sugar, you make my soul complete. Rapture tastes so sweet." That's from the same trance tune I mentioned. It's sung by Nadia Ali, from Pakistan.

I CALLED ROZ and left a message asking if she'd like to come by and help me shampoo the dog. The flea shampoo is turquoise with sparkles and very thick. It's really a two-person job to put it on—one person to work in the suds and one person to hold Smacko's back and aim the shower sprayer. He keeps wanting to shake, spraying turquoise froth everywhere, and he will shake, unless one person keeps a steady, firm hand on the middle of his back.

Roz called and said she'd be by at about six-thirty. I knew she would—she misses the dog like crazy, and who can blame her? I got out some chips and salsa and was sitting in the white plastic chair by the barn door when she drove up. I watched her walk up the driveway, looking very calm and elegant in her dog-washing outfit of jeans and a loose blue shirt with a paint splash on the sleeve. She stopped and said hello to Smacko and picked up something in the sand. I heard her bracelets jingle, a sound I hadn't heard in a while. "Here's a present from the driveway," she said, and she handed it to me. It was a fragment of old china with very fine rule-lines in blue against white. Bits of old china sometimes appear in the driveway as rains wash more of its sand away. I took off my glasses to look at it and thanked her. Then I offered her a chip.

We washed the dog and didn't get too wet, and then she said she had to go. I asked her if maybe she'd like to stay and watch *Bull Durham* with me. She likes *Bull Durham*.

"Is it done?" she asked, meaning the introduction.

"It is not done. Nor will it ever be done, for I am not the one to do it."

"Oh, poof," she said. "You just need to apply yourself."

She didn't leave right away, at least. She smiled at the tablecloth. On it was my paperback of Mary Oliver's *New and Selected Poems, Volume 1*—I seem to be carrying it around the house with me. "So that's what she looks like," Roz said, tilting her head to see the picture on the cover better. It's the blue-tinted photograph in which Mary is wearing some kind of wonderful ulster with a zippered hood, and she's looking off, and she looks heartstoppingly French. "She's beautiful," Roz said. "Is that a recent picture?"

She's about seventy now, I said, and living in Provincetown.

"Is she lesbian?"

I said I believed she was, yes.

"It's odd that the woman I most want to look like is a lesbian," she said. Then she said a long goodbye to Smacko and we hugged ceremonially and she drove away.

I didn't want to watch *Bull Durham,* so I watched three episodes of *The Dick Van Dyke Show.* Three's about my limit for one night.

GENE'S NEW EMAIL says that they're becoming "really concerned." I feel horrible about it. I don't want to disappoint him. Gene, I'm sorry. I apologize for this inexcusable slowness.

If I could just die and rot in the ground it would be okay. I wouldn't have to write anything more. Die and rot and be completely dead. No worries. Everything's good. "Paul Chowder was at work on an anthology of rhyming poetry when he died." "Ah, too bad."

The best use of the word "rot" that I can think of is from a poem by Coventry Patmore. He's sitting in a bay.

He's just had some reversal, we're not sure what. The ocean and its waves are out there. He looks at them. What kind of ocean is it? It's a "purposeless, glad ocean." That's what first caught me, those two words, "purposeless" and "glad," placed together. But then comes the next stanza, which is a killer. Suddenly he raises his voice and he says, "The lie shall rot."

> When all its work is done, the lie shall rot;
> The truth is great, and shall prevail,
> When none cares whether it prevail or not.

I know I'll never write anything anywhere near as good as that eight-line poem by Coventry Patmore. Which is in many, many anthologies. I've sailed past fifty and I've had my chances and it hasn't happened.

But there's still the hope that leaps. There's still the tiny possibility. You think: One more poem. You think: There will be some as yet ungathered anthology of American poetry. It will be the anthology that people will tote around with them on subways thirty-five, forty years from now. There will be many new names in its table of contents—poets who are only children now, or aren't known. And you think: Maybe this very poem I write today will somehow pry open a space in that future anthology and maybe it will drop into position and root itself there.

I guess that probably explains why I used to collect anthologies. I was hoping to find a crack in the pavement where my ailanthus of a poem could take root.

IT WAS ABOUT MIDNIGHT and misty after another brief rain. I wanted to sit in the white plastic chair by the driveway and admire the overboiled potato of the moon, but I knew that the basin of the chair would be filled with water. So I tipped the chair forward, in the dark, with the crickets going, and I could hear a splash as the water poured into the grass. I hesitated for an instant, wondering whether it was worth my while to sit myself down in the wet chair and get my pants wet. And my answer was immediately yes. Of course I wanted to sit in the wet chair. No sacrifice is too great. And meanwhile the mist came up the hill and a wild turkey was peeling out a great crazy screeching cry down by the creek. He's lost, or he's lost someone, or he's having an argument or an orgasm. I'm breathing the same mist that the turkey screeched into—the same mist that has boiled away the moon.

Out of the corner of my eye I saw a firefly inscribe part of a curve, and I remembered W. S. Merwin's poem "To The Corner of the Eye." I thought: It is so, so good to know that W. S. Merwin exists. I even love his initials. W. and S.—ideal initials. Merwin writes poems that, fortunately, I can't remember. They would be exceedingly difficult to memorize. But imagine being the poetry editor, maybe at *The New Yorker,* getting "To the Corner of the Eye" in the mail and reading it. Imagine how thrilledly shaken up you would feel at reading it and knowing that you had the power to publish it. Although come to think of it, "To the Corner of the Eye" wasn't published in *The New Yorker*.

Then, in the mist, I saw a big man walking up the street. He was wearing one shoe. He had a familiar look, so I got out of my chair and went partway down the driveway, and I waved at him. It's not usual, really, for people to walk up and down my street without two shoes on at midnight. He stopped. He put his hand on the telephone pole that's there. He looked down. And then he looked over at me. He was a big guy. Big strong bald head. Wide nose. Kind of a defiant, wild, defeated look. I said, "Ted? Ted Roethke? Is that you?" And he nodded slightly. I said, "Wow, Ted, how's it going? You look like you just got hit with a couple hundred million volts of electricity."

"No, it's hydrotherapy," he said. " 'I do not laugh, I do not cry; / I'm sweating out the will to die.' "

"Whoa, Ted," I said. "Sounds a little like Dr. Seuss, except dark. You want to come in and maybe make a phone call to a loved one?"

He shook his head no. I went back to my chair and sat down. The mist came and went. In ten minutes, a car pulled up behind him, and a man got out and led him into the car, and they drove away.

I went inside, and I got in bed next to some anthologies and W. S. Merwin's *The Vixen* and slept quite well.

W. S. MERWIN SAID his mother read poetry to him. Well, mine did, too. Several times my mother read me Shelley's poem "Ozymandias." Percy Shelley, played by William Shatner, is riding in some caravan across a mental desert, and he comes to two enormous carved ankles and calves that tower above him. "Look on my works, ye mighty, and despair," say the words carved into the pedestal, in some lost language. Carl Orff's *Carmina Burana* is playing its great hollow choral chords in the background, as it always does.

My mother came to the last line. She read, "The lone and level sands stretch far away." Present tense. An instance, there, of the necessary compression and deformation of speech: "lone" doesn't quite make sense. Shelley had in mind the isolated, the forlorn, the lonely, ruined, sandy scene—but the meter called for one syllable, and so he wrote "lone," which is perfect. Lone and level.

I have to warn you, though: There is a most painful enjambment in "Ozymandias." Because of this one enjambment, I can almost not bear to read the poem as printed on its page. Which is another good argument for memorizing— if you memorize, you can loop through just the parts of a poem you like, without having the flawed lines flaunt themselves for your eye.

What is enjambment? Enjambment is the key to the whole conundrum. The word originally comes from an old

French word, *"jambon."* "Jambon" means ham. Anytime Ronsard or one of those French troubador poets used enjambment, they flung a slice of ham at him. Ronsard learned his lesson and wrote some really nice love songs.

No, very briefly, enjambment is a word that means that you're wending your way along a line of poetry, and you're walking right out to the very end of the line, way out, and it's all going fine, and you're expecting the syntax to give you a polite tap on the shoulder to wait for a moment. Just a second, sir, or madam, while we rhyme, or come to the end of our phrasal unit, or whatever. While we rest. But instead the syntax pokes at you and says hustle it, pumpkin, keep walking, don't rest. So naturally, because you're stepping out onto nothingness, you fall. You tumble forward, gaaaah, and you end up all discombobulated at the beginning of the next line, with a banana peel on your head and some coffee grounds in your shirt pocket. In other words, you're "jammed" into the next line—that's what enjambment is. So in the case of "Ozymandias," second line, you've got "Two vast and trunkless legs of stone"—end of line, we need to pause, but no, keep moving, woopsie doodle, next line—"*Stand* in the desert." Ouch.

THERE ARE TWO KINDS of enjambment. There's regular enjambment, which is part of traditional poetry and is almost always a bad idea, but especially in sonnets—and then there's what's known as ultra-extreme enjambment. Ultra-extreme enjambment comes standard in free verse because free verse is, as we know, merely a heartfelt arrangement of plummy words requesting to be read slowly. So you can break the line anywhere you want. In fact you want to

> break against any
> moments of natural

> pause, not with
> them, to keep

everyone on their toes and off balance. So at the end of a line, you might find a word like "the" that requires another word to go along with it. That's how you know that you're in the middle of an ultra-extreme enjambment situation. And you know you're in trouble if that's not what you're looking for. But if that is what you're looking for, then it's fine and you're happy. And there are many poems that enjamb all over themselves, that I love.

SOMEDAY, when I feel you're ready, I will show you *The Vixen*, by W. S. Merwin. Here it is, in fact. Got it right here in a pile, surprise surprise. That's a photo of a vixen in the snow on the cover—in other words, a fox. The title poem isn't the best poem in the book. So often true.

W. S. Merwin was one of these guys who—well, he wanted to be a poet, and he thought that Ezra Pound was the modernist man, the founder of it all. Which he was. So in the forties Merwin went and visited Ezra Pound in the insane asylum, where Pound was hanging out, doing rather well. Many aspiring poets would go to St. Elizabeths, outside D.C., and visit Pound and listen to him ramble on. They'd bring him gifts of tea and cookies and tins of jellied ox tongue and whatnot. He was a celebrity, an oracle—and if you wanted to be a certain kind of poet you went to visit him in the booby hatch to say hello to the maestro. Dorothy, his wife, would be there, making sure everything went all right, steering him away from his fixed idées. Pound, who was by nature a blustering bigot—a humorless jokester—a talentless pasticheur—a confidence man—was now supported by the American state. He had a sinecure. He'd spent the war being paid by Mussolini's press bureau to say things on shortwave radio like "the kikes have sucked out your vitals." And bad things about Roosevelt. Pound admired Mussolini and Hitler—he'd admired them both long before the war. So when the Americans took control of Italy he was arrested and held in solitary confinement. Archibald MacLeish, who'd read the transcripts of the broadcasts, wrote letters to the attorney general to get him sprung. Eventually Pound ended up back in the United States, and MacLeish got him a good lawyer and a good shrink and saved him from being tried for treason, on the grounds that he was mentally "unsound."

Why? Because the modern movement was too precious

to suffer that kind of public discrediting. If Pound were tried for treason, the damning transcripts of his broadcasts would be all over the papers. MacLeish himself might have to testify. Modernism would have a big black eye. The ugliness of its Futurist-fascist patrimony would be exposed. T. S. Eliot would look bad. In fact, Pound might be sentenced to death, as Lord Haw-Haw was, though not by hanging. Lord Haw-Haw was hung. No, Pound had to be packed safely away in the excelsior of St. Elizabeths, where his legend could accrete. In fact, MacLeish and Eliot and Allen Tate engineered a special new poetry prize for him, the Bollingen Prize, to clean up his image.

So now Pound was safe, and he became the cracker-barrel philosopher of free verse. People made pilgrimages. And he loved telling them what to do. That had always been his great talent. He'd told Yeats what to do—he'd presided over Yeats's Monday night get-togethers in London, handing out the cigarettes and the cheese doodles and telling Yeats that his late writing was "putrid." And he'd told T. S. Eliot what all to cut from "The Waste Land," and he'd told Hilda Doolittle how to fix her poems, and he'd told Harriet Monroe, the editor of *Poetry* magazine in Chicago, whom she should publish in her magazine—he was *Poetry*'s official foreign correspondent for a while, and he scolded Harriet and her colleague Alice when they went soft and published the occasional piece of Sara Teasdalian verse. He'd even told Amy Lowell what to do, until she finally got tired of his high-horsing and took herself and her cigar box elsewhere. Then Pound and Wyndham Lewis started a new movement, Vorticism, which was Futurism by a different name. It was hard, cruel, pitiless, strong. It was pre-fascist, in fact. The first poem in the first issue of *BLAST,* the Vorticist periodical, had a line in it, later altered. The line was: "Let us be done with Jews." Written by: Ezra Pound. By then London hated Pound, for good reason, and he moved to Paris to tell James Joyce how to fix *Ulysses.* Yeats's father said, "Hatred is the harvest he wants to gather."

And even decades later, after the Second World War was done, people went to Pound for advice—crazy people like Charles Olson and nice people like Bill Merwin, who in 1948 had no notion of the fierceness of Pound's lifelong disorientations and his hatreds. Pound gave them all advice. And some of it was good advice.

POUND'S ADVICE to Bill Merwin was: You've got to do translations. Sharpen your mind with translations. So Merwin did a lot of translations. He translated from the Spanish and the French and from the Russian, and rare bits from the Welsh and the Eskimo. Really worked at it, for years. And I don't know if it was good for him or not to translate so much, but the upshot of it all was that he wrote a beautiful book of poems late in life called *The Vixen.* And another beautiful book called *Present Company.*

Merwin is a fairly old man now. He lives in Hawaii, where he, I think, cultivates rare forms of palm tree. Or is it pineapple tree? Anyway he does something rare with botany. In Hawaii. Still sharp as anything.

I miss my mom and dad.

So many poets are disappointments when you hear them talk on the radio. But Merwin isn't like that. I heard him talk once while I was on the Portsmouth rotary, and I missed my turnoff onto Route 16 and went all the way around again, and now every time I go around that rotary I think of Merwin's voice on the radio. He's got a wise sensibleness and a gentleness of inflection that makes you want to listen. And all the poems in his book *The Vixen* have the same form, which is that one line goes along for about ten words, and then it enjambs into the next line, which is indented, and that line goes along, and it enjambs into the next line, which begins at the left margin. And then indented. And then left margin, and then indented. So each of the poems has this very consistent square-toothed edge. And there's no punctuation, none, so you have to figure out where the long sentences begin or end. That's part of the joy of it, in fact, that you don't know sometimes whether a word is part of the end of one idea or the beginning of the next idea. Everything enjambs visually until you read it aloud to yourself and hear where the breaks should come.

There's a nice one about a lizard, and one about a door with a worn threshold, and one about a woman who has a plum tree that grows a certain kind of plum called a "mirabelle." All Merwin's poems in this book are good, practically every one.

7

I HAVE TO GIVE a reading in Cambridge soon.

Elizabeth Bishop gave her first reading in 1947 at Wellesley. "I was sick for days ahead of time," she said. And then she gave another reading in 1949, and she was sick again beforehand, and nobody in the audience could hear her. And then she didn't give any readings for twenty-six years after that. Isn't that a revealing fact? And then somehow she found that she could do it—she had less stage fright.

If you listen to those late readings, you can hear the greater confidence and authority in her voice. And the age. Her voice is lower and slower and surer. She's probably had a drink or two to fortify herself. Whatever it is, she does very well at reading late in life. The audience loves her, and they laugh. She reads them the poem about the filling station, which appeared in *The New Yorker* and in the big yellow *New Yorker Book of Poems*.

I went back up to the second floor of the barn and I sat in the white plastic chair and I sweated, because it's hot, and I thought: You can't force it. If it isn't there you can't force it. Then I thought: You can force it. My whole life I've been forcing it. You throw yourself against the weight of the massive sliding door to the barn, that does not want to move, and you lean and you wag your hips and you haul on the metal handle, and you strain, and you grunt, and you point your face at the sky and say bad words, and it starts to move and rumble, and then it moves a little more easily, and then a little more easily still, and finally, the barn door is open wide enough that you barely fit through, taking care not to scrape your back on the broken-off lock flange.

So you can force it, and you should force it. All the time. Force it open. Push. Pull. When you think you can't, think again. On the other hand, sometimes the wood of the door is a little rotten around the handle and you tear out the screws. My father was right. Sometimes the door is really just stuck.

THE EMPTINESS of this floor of the barn is its greatest quality. This barn is, I guess you could say, my family barn. My parents bought this house in 1961, when I was still a kid.

There's a house, an ell, which is the connecting structure, and the barn. They put a new roof on the barn, which is really all you need to do. You need to keep the rain out. As soon as a roof starts to leak, the decay, the collapse, the inner fungosity take charge. You've got to have a roof on your barn. I see it over and over again, the slumping to the side. "Two more payments and it's ours"—that postcard.

The first floor is a chaos, and I've been filling it with even more boxes. It's a madhouse of stored boxes. But the second floor is still quite empty. Well, right now it has the folding table with sections of my anthology on it. But it's almost empty. It will be empty again. Broom clean, as they say in real estate.

My broom is rotten. Over the winter, it became a blackened side-swerving dense stump. It was almost unrecognizable. It had literally decayed. You simply cannot leave a corn broom outside over the winter. I don't know what I was thinking. I was distracted, I guess—by the anthology and by money and by things going wrong with Roz. Once I wiped snow off the windshield and then I just carelessly leaned it against the house and then a fallen roof drift covered it. What a mistake. It's downright painful to try to sweep with this moist stump of a broom.

I called Tim and I said, "I'm just very worried that they may have stopped making brooms like this, because people all seem to own little plastic brooms now."

Tim said that he was pretty sure that he'd seen similar

classic corn brooms for sale at Target recently. So I went to Target, to the broom aisle, and Tim was absolutely right. I'd just assumed that the old style wouldn't be there anymore, but it was. It's made by the Libman Company, and it's still made in the United States. I came home, and I tore off the plastic, and there was the same smocking, the same tight spiral of shiny wire. I slid aside the doormat and whistled at all the sand that had collected under there, and I swept it clean away.

Then I drove to Roz's place to tell her that I'd gotten a new broom. I saw her getting out of a car with a man. She was dressed up. Cripe. And yet of course she should. If you break up with someone then you go out with someone else.

While I was gone the mouse in the kitchen found half an old cookie and tried to pull it up into the stove's control panel, which is where he lives. But the cookie wouldn't fit. So he just ate it where it was. Ate and shat discreetly and had quite a little party.

I MADE AN EGG SALAD SANDWICH and took a bite of it over the open silverware drawer. A piece of egg salad fell in among the forks. I swore softly with my mouth full. Another piece of egg salad fell in. At first I was going to leave the bits there and then I thought, No, you have to keep on top of things, and I dabbed them up. Then I wiped some of the night's kinked mouse droppings from the stovetop.

Then I thought of a poet named Ed Ochester. Good poet. And then I thought of another good poet, Mary Kinzie. And then I thought of another one, Matthew Rohrer. And another, Stanley Plumly. There are hundreds of poets like Ed O. And like me. And we all love the busy ferment, and we all know it's nonsense. Getting together for conferences of international poetry. Hah! A joke. Reading our poems. Our little moment. Physical presence. In the same room with. A community. Forget it. It's a joke.

But then one day you open up a book to a certain page, and you read, "Up from the bronze, I saw / Water without a flaw"—Louise Bogan's "Roman Fountain." And you see why it's all necessary, the whole enterprise. *Water without a flaw.* My life is necessary because I sustain the idea of poetry through thick and thin. That's my job.

What does it mean to be a great poet? It means that you wrote one or two great poems. Or great parts of poems. That's all it means. Don't try to picture the waste or it will alarm you. Even in a big life like Louise Bogan's or Theodore Roethke's. The two of them had an affair, as I said. They had a busy weekend with many cries of pleasure, and it helped their writing a lot. Or Howard Moss's life, or Swinburne's life, or Tennyson's life—any poet's life. Out of hundreds of poems two or three are really good. Maybe four or five. Six tops. All the middling poems they write are necessary to form a raised mulch bed or nest for the great poems and to prove to the world that they labored diligently and in good faith for some years at their calling. In other words, they can't just dash off one or two great poems and then stop. That won't work. Nobody will give them the "great poet" label if they write just two great poems and nothing else. Even if they're the greatest poems ever. But it's perfectly okay, in fact it's typical, if ninety-five percent of the poems they write aren't great. Because they never are.

A lifetime of fretting over pieces of paper and this is what you've got. And yet it's worth it, isn't it? That's what you have to think. All the chewing of salad, the eating of pickled beets and the little marinated ears of corn, those flexible baby corn ears, and the waitress coming by saying, "Folks, how is everything?" You nod and smile gratefully, chewing. "Can I get you another Smuttynose?" Sure, I'll take another.

TENNYSON'S AT THE SALAD BAR, making his way around, holding the chilled plastic plate, fumbling in his beard. Poet laureate of the British empire. Staring for a long time at the tub of bean salad. Corn salad or bean salad, which will it be today? "Into the valley of death, rode the six hundred!" Plop—beans. Pope's there. Alexander Pope, the magpie trickster rockpolisher. Malevolently ladling the blue cheese at eye level. Taking care not to spill. Hey, Alex! You don't want to talk to me? That's fine.

And what each of them comes up with is a couple of pages' worth of poems in an anthology. All of that rhythmic chewing and swallowing and digesting, all the conversational nodding—"Yes, yes, true, true, mm-hm"—results in something called *Collected Poems,* and out of those collected poems grow a few sprouts, a couple of pages in a paperback.

That's the way it works. Long ago there was an article in *Commentary.* The article was called "Why We Need More Waste, Fraud, and Mismanagement in the Pentagon." The idea was that in order to build a magnificent weapon of deterrence, you need to tolerate twenty-dollar screws and five-hundred-dollar screwdrivers. Well, it's not really true of the Pentagon. But it's true of poetry.

We honestly don't need more fraud and waste in the Pentagon. We need to retrain some of the weapons engineers, so that they can teach high school. Some of them might write light verse. We might have a sudden upwelling of light verse. I mean, God, what has happened that we have no good light verse? Practically none. It's shocking. It's tragic. *The New Yorker* used to publish light verse in every issue. Newman Levy's verse. Newman Levy, the lawyer poet. And of course Ogden Nash. Roethke published some light verse. So did Updike. Now nothing. Hip-hop is our light verse, I guess. Some of it's quick and clever, and some of it isn't.

An American man wrote up his memories of Tennyson a hundred years ago in *The Century* magazine. Tennyson told him that one of the best lines he wrote was about the French Revolution: "Freedom free to slay herself, and dying while they shout her name." Which is a good line.

Tennyson also said, to this man, that he didn't want any biography of him written: "I don't want to be ripped up like a hog when I'm dead."

I DECIDED TO TAKE the white plastic chair down to the creek. There's a creek at the bottom of the hill of sand on which my house sits. I had the chair in my hand, and I had my gear and my Sharpies and my presentation easel for practicing, and I looked as if I was prepared for an expedition up the Orinoco. I was about to turn down the hill when I heard tires on my driveway. It was my neighbor Nan's yellow Subaru. I peered toward her car and thought I could see her face and through the branchy reflection a wave, maybe a nervous wave, I don't know, and then her window came down. She said, "Are you off somewhere with your white chair?"

I said that I was going down to the creek to think over the origins of rhyme.

"Would you be interested in a chicken leg?" Nan asked. She said that she did Meals on Wheels once a week, and she had an extra meal because someone had been away at a doctor's appointment. She got it out of the box in the back seat and showed it to me. It was an orange piece of chicken in a segmented tray with a sheet of plastic glued over it. There were secondary pockets, each shaped like lungs, one of which had yellow pieces of corn pointing in all directions, and one of which had beans pointing in all directions.

"Mmmm," I said. "Don't you want it?"

Nan said she didn't want it. "Would you care for the slice of bread and the carton of milk, too?"

I said yes indeed I would.

She got in her car and began backing away. "Enjoy yourself!"

I waved and stuck the Meals on Wheels meal into my equipment bag, at an angle, and tucked the bag of milk and a roll in another place. Then I carried my white plastic chair down through the patch of skunk cabbage to the creek and put it right in the water and sat down on it. Immediately the rear chair legs worked their way down through the mud, and I sank an inch.

The spring floods have changed everything, as they generally do, and so I'm sitting now at the base of carved-away banks that are about five feet high, looking up at the undersides of ferns. There are innumerable ferns.

Why is rhyme so important to speech?

I think I'm going to give this chicken a try.

Wow, it's fantastic. Meals on Wheels chicken. Fantastically good. Fleshy as hell, though. The flight muscles of a bird. Think of it. Wash it down with a little milk, strange as that may seem. Mmm. Excuse me.

And there's a piece of bread in waxed paper, with a pat of margarine, dyed very yellow. Not bad. Honestly, the chicken and the bread are so good that I wonder how the corn and the beans can top them. But maybe they will.

Beans are good. Corn is good. My first Meals on Wheels meal. What does that mean? Is Nan worried about me? Does she feel sorry for me? Does she think I'm an old guy?

There's an incredible amount of pollen blowing sideways past my face. I can see it sometimes. Hundreds of thousands of little grains on their way somewhere.

QUITE QUICKLY after you're born you begin to suck. The sucking teaches you some lessons. First, that if you pull your tongue back a certain way, a warm delicious liquid that is not your own saliva flows into your mouth. And second, that your tongue is an unusually important muscle.

So you exercise your tongue, and it gets stronger and more aware of what it can do. That's the first order of business. And then when you plop off the nipple, you look up, and what's waiting for you there? Two huge amazing wonderful shiny things. Your mother's eyes. And below that is a strange item with two nostril holes, and then there's a single large flexible opening at the bottom, which moves around a lot in an interesting way, and out of it issues all this marvelous taffylike goopy stuff that you can't see but that goes into your ears. It's impossible to make sense of it, but it's nice, and you like it. Something deep in you tells you to listen to it. It's speech. And when your mom's mouth smiles you learn the color white.

The mouth says, "A boo boo boo! Yes, my little fumble

nuggets! A noo noo noo!" Aiming the sound at you. Talking to you, in other words, in a particular tone of voice. And thoughtful people have studied this tone of voice, and they understand that this is not something to be lightly dismissed. This talk is the crucial ingredient. This is the way that the genetic memory of speech is being imprinted on a new practitioner.

Baby talk, which is full of rhyme, is really the way you learn to figure out what's like and what's not like, and what is a discrete word, or an utterance, and what is just a transition between two words.

How does it happen? Well, it happens gradually, and it happens by matching. Matching within and matching without. First you have to learn that a certain feeling in one part of your body, your tongue, matches with a certain feeling in your brain, which is a sound. A slightly different feeling in your tongue matches with a different sound coming out of your mouth and a different sensation of muscular control registering in your brain. Each subtle difference of sound feels different. And this is all very difficult and takes lots of trial and error and babbling and drooling and lip popping and laughing.

Of course, you're doing a lot of random sudden things at that point. Your eyes dart left. Your fist suddenly goes boing! Sticks out. Head swivels. Whoa. Back arch. Leg. Sudden diaper squirt. Things are happening everywhere. And each one of the things that happen, the random little twitchy things, sends a message to central control that feels a certain way. So you begin to correlate. And your mouth turns out to be probably the most important piece of the pie. When you cry you get results, and when you suck you get milk, and when you go "Nnnnnng!" the face above you smiles and goes " 'Nnnnng,' what do you mean 'Nnng,' you funny little baby?" Reflecting it back.

And you start to see that all these sounds that you can make—ngo, merk, plort—that you begin to hear, can be classified in certain ways. You're a newborn brain, you've only recently come out of solitary confinement in the uterus, and you're already a cryptanalyst in Bletchley Park. You're already parsing through, looking for similarities and differences, looking for patterns, looking for beginnings and endings and hints of meaning.

ESPECIALLY BEGINNINGS. The beginning of a sound is usually a moment where you forbid the sound to be produced. With your lips. Puh, buh, bluh. Or you attempt to dissuade it gently: nnn, mmmm. You put some sort of barrier or seawall there, and then you remove it to allow the sound to unfold itself briskly into a vowel. Unfold the vowel towel and floom it out and let it settle on the sand. Flume, broom, room, spume, gloom, doom.

So you've got the beginning, which is generally a consonant, and then you've got the middle of the sound, which is often a vowelly region. And then you've got the end of the sound. And all these things are difficult to make out. We know from speech-recognition software how hard it is for a computer to figure out where things begin and end. It's like looking at the horizon and thinking, Is that lump Mount Monadnock or is Mount Monadnock that lump there? Actually Mount Monadnock is pretty distinctive. But sometimes when you look at a mountain range it's very difficult to know what's what.

Do you care how things are spelled? Obviously not. Spelling? What's that? That's absurdity. That's a whole different layer of opacity—the layer of squirming black shapes on a page. That's years in the future. What you're doing, inside your head, is classing things by sound shape. And by detachable head. And that's where rhyme comes in.

Think of what happens when you say the word "moon." What does the speech part of your brain do? It says, Okay, assignment: moon. Jaw down a bit, lips together. And flatten. Good. Then commence huffing out some sound. Constrict the vocal cords. Mm. Now open and flute the lips into an O shape. Ooo. Moo. And then terminate by flipping up the bottom of the tongue and lightly caressing the roof of the mouth. Airtight seal. And out the nose. Moon—ah. And you're done.

That's all your mouth control center knows. It knows a series of muscular commands. It does not know spelling or meaning. And because it's an efficient mouth control center, it classes that series of muscular commands as being very similar to one next door to it: rune. The end is the same, and it's going to store that near "moon," but it's going to give you a different beginning. It's going to say, Okay, go back in the back of your mouth, I want you to do something kind of difficult with the back of your tongue. And then I want you to flip your tongue up. Rrr. Don't roll it! Don't roll the R, don't trill it, because you are not Sarah Bernhardt. You're not William Butler Yeats. You're just going to say "rune."

The tongue is a rhyming fool. It wants to rhyme because that's how it stores what it knows. It's got a detailed checklist of muscle moves for every consonant and vowel and diphthong and fricative and flap and plosive. Pull, relax, twitch, curl, touch. And somewhere in there, on some neural net in your underconsciousness, stored away, all these checklists, or neuromuscular profiles, or call them sound curves, are stored away, like the parts of car bodies, or spoons, with similar shapes nested near each other. Broom and loom and tomb and spume and womb and whom are all lying there on the table in one spot. And you figured all that out by yourself. They rhyme.

And what's different about them? The all-important beginning. The removable hair. Or the wig. The sound has a body, a sort of a snaky thing, with a little bell on its tail. And then when you get up to the head, the head can have a bunch of puffy P kind of hair on its head, poom, or a fluffy FL kind of hair, or a dark black M hairdo, or big blowsy bastardizing hair. You can have all kinds of hair preceding that oom sound.

Buh. Hoo. Huh. Hay. And once you've got them classed and labeled, you can start taking off and putting on the sound-wigs. You pick up "plume" and you carefully, patiently, take off the PL and you put it aside. Don't drop it! And you pick up the BL, put that on. Get it properly adjusted. Brrrrrr. Brrrrroooom.

So what rhyming poems do is they take all these nearby sound curves and remind you that they first existed that way in your brain. Before they meant something specific, they had a shape and a way of being said. And now, yes, gloom and broom are floating fifty miles away from each other in your mind because they refer to different notions, but they're cheek-by-jowl as far as your tongue is concerned. And that's what a poem does. Poems match sounds up the way you matched them when you were a tiny kid, using that detachable front phoneme. They're saying, That way that you first learned language, right at the beginning, by hearing what was similar and what was different, and figuring it all out all by yourself, that way is still important. You're going to hear it, and you're going to like it. It's going to pull you back to the beginning of speech.

And that's why we like puns, too. Some puns. A few puns. Orange you glad. Puns and plays and near-misses and alliterations. Fair and foul. Fee fie fo fum. Liquor locker. The Quicker Picker Upper. Road rage. Boxtop. Pickpocket. Smile and dial. Drink and drive. Lip-smacking, whip-cracking Cracker Jacks.

Or: Sir, isn't that a steering wheel sticking out of your zipper? Yes, it's driving me nuts.

We like to visit the parallel sound-studio universe with all these mixing boards and XLR patch cables going here and there, independent of the other part of our head, which is the conscious part that has spent a long time sweating the books and trying to make sense of objects and ideas and meanings. Trying to be a responsible citizen.

Rhyme taught us to talk.

I RANG NAN'S DOORBELL and told her how good the chicken was, and she said she was glad to hear it. But she seemed a little preoccupied, maybe even a little down. She said that she'd just gotten two very high estimates to put in a wide plank floor in her guest room—both more than twenty-eight hundred dollars.

"To nail in a pine plank floor?" I said, exaggerating my incredulity. "Well, blow me down. I'll do it for you at cost."

She said no, no, that was impossible—and anyway did I know how to install floors? Which was a legitimate question in the circumstances. I said that yes, I did know how to install floors, if by "floors" you didn't mean hardwood floors. I'd installed the plank floor in my ell with my dad a few decades ago. And I've done a little light cabinetwork over the years, I added modestly. "You have to allow a little space at the ends for expansion, that's all."

She considered. "I'd have to pay you, otherwise it's awkward."

"Pay me fifteen dollars an hour. I'm not a real carpenter. We can do it together. Your son can help."

She looked at me for a while and then she smiled. Would I like to come over later and measure the room?

I said I would.

8

MAYBE I COULD DO a weekly podcast. Play some theme music, maybe Root Boy Slim singing "Put a Quarter in the Juke," and then: Hello, this is Paul Chowder welcoming you to Chowder's Bowl of Poetry. And I'm your host, Paul Chowder, and this is Chowder's Plumfest of Poems. Hello, and welcome to the Paul Chowder Poetry Hour. I'm your host and confidant, Paul Chowder, and I'd like to welcome you to Chowder's Flying Spoonful of Rhyme. And this is Chowder's Poetry Cheatsheet, and I'm your host, Paul Chowder, from hell and gone, welcoming you to Chowder's Thimblesquirt of Verse.

I could never keep it up. You have to hand it to those podcasters. They keep on going week after week, even though nobody's listening to them. And then eventually they puff up and die.

Let's begin today, however, by talking about the history of rhyme. If you're prepared, I'm prepared. Actually I'm not all that prepared, because when I'm prepared that's when I fail. I learn too much and it crowds out what I actually know. There's crammer's knowledge and then there's knowledge that is semipermanent.

So the first thing about the history of rhyme, and the all-important Rhymesters' Rebellion of 1697, is that it's all happened before. It's all part of these huge rhymeorhythmic circles of exuberance and innovation and surfeit and decay and resurrectional primitivism and waxing sophistication and infill and overgrowth and too much and we can't stand it and let's stop and do something else.

LET'S TRY AGAIN. The history of poetry began, quite possibly, in the year 1883. Let me write that date for you with my Sharpie, so you can have it for your convenience. 1883. That's when it all began. Or maybe not. Could be any year. The year doesn't matter. Forget the year! The important thing is that there's something called the nineteenth century, which is like a huge forest of old-growth birch and beech. That's what they used to make clothespins out of, birch and beech. New England was the clothespin-manufacturing capital of the world. There was a factory in Vanceborough, Maine, that made eight hundred clothespins a minute in 1883. Those clothespins went out to England, to France, to Spain, to practically every country in the world. Clothes in every country were stretched out on rope to dry in the sun and held in place by New England clothespins. Elizabeth Barrett Browning probably used New England clothespins. I'm not kidding.

And the way that we write the nineteenth century on a piece of paper is we go "19" and then we do a special little thing on top. A nifty little thing that's sort of like a little bug flying around the nineteenth century. And that's called the "th." It means "nineteenth" century. And that's how we abbreviate the enormity of what happened.

But here's a tip. If you say "nineteen hundreds" when you mean "nineteenth century," you're going to get in trouble with your dates. Because the nineteenth century is the eighteen hundreds. But! Don't say "the eighteen hundreds." People who say "the eighteen hundreds" are looked at in a special way by the people who say "the nineteenth century." The people who use eighteen hundreds don't know that. They don't know that the people who say "nineteenth century" are looking askance at them. So please consider not saying "eighteen hundreds," because the people who say "nineteenth century" will dismiss what you have to say. You can refer very knowingly to a specific decade *of* the nineteenth century— you can say, for instance, "the eighteen-eighties," or even, extra-knowingly, "the eighties"—but never "the eighteen hundreds."

So it's the nineteenth century we're talking about today. And on a timeline, it goes all the way from here—to here. Exactly one hundred years of pure poetry. And in that space of time, a lot happened. And after that time, in what is called the twentieth century, events became quite confused and nobody knew what they were doing. Rhyme went all to hell, and everything became a jumble.

And that's why we like to talk about the nineteenth century, because it's more fun, and everybody knows names like Byron, Shelley, Keats, Coleridge—and Swinburne. And Tennyson. And Mr. Browning. And Mrs. Browning. And Arnold. And Emily Dickinson, of course. And Longfellow. And a bunch of other poets. The names just go on and on, because the nineteenth century was the century of English poetry. Coterminous with the flowering of the British empire was the flowering of the empire of English verse. And that is not what we will be talking about today.

Today we will just be talking about this moment right here. Right at the very end of the nineteenth century. The ends of centuries have a special meaning, as everybody who moves slowly toward them knows. Who was alive at the very end of the nineteenth cenury, at this last fleeting moment? Well, Swinburne was still alive. He was deaf, but he was still alive.

And there were some younger people chiming in. There

were some people like Kipling. And Henley. And Patmore. And Alice Meynell. And Edmund Gosse. Gosse had met Tennyson and Swinburne, and he visited Walt Whitman before he died. He found Whitman sitting in an upstairs room in New Jersey. Clippings from various articles about himself were scattered on the floor. Every so often Whitman would fish up an article about himself and read a bit of it aloud.

So there was a lot going on there in the nineteenth century. And they lived their lives, and they wrote some poems, and then suddenly they bumped into the end of it. And they blasted through into 1901. That was the big moment, because then there they were in the twentieth century. When you're in the twentieth century, it's a whole different ball game. There are huge tropical plants dripping raw latex. There are giant pieces of diesel-powered earth-moving equipment. Turbines, huge hydroelectric projects. There's dynamite blowing up over there. There are exotic shores that are lapped at by alien warm pale-blue crinkled Saran Wrap sheets of ocean. There's neon, of course. Italy is a mess. Switzerland—who knows? France is a question mark. As is Austro-Hungary. It's all up for grabs! And who conquers the twentieth century? Who takes it from here on in and says, I've got it, folks? I'll take care of it, you don't have to worry about it now. Who takes care of it? I'll tell you who. The worst possible person, unfortunately. His name was Marinetti. The leader of the Futurists. Filippo Tommaso Marinetti. Manic Phil, who marinated the twentieth century in his influence. Marinetti was aggressive, he wanted to change things, and he wanted to break things. He wanted old buildings leveled. He wanted Venice blown up. He was a great writer of manifestos. Or manifesti.

And one morning in 1909, Marinetti's Futurist manifesto was published in Paris. The intellectuals opened the *Figaro* that morning, and there was this full page of authoritative promulgations. That said that the past was to be jettisoned. That Europe needed a new way of thinking. It was time to embrace steam and speed and power and war. The old ways were no good. Marinetti didn't use the word "fascism," but that's what it led to. Futurism led directly to Mussolini and Hitler. It also led to modern poetry. The two roads diverged, but not so much. There was in Marinetti's modernism a desire to stomp around heedlessly and a wish to sweep the counter clean. The ambitious guy poets really liked Marinetti.

And some of the girl poets liked the guy poets. Mina Loy, for example—that brilliant strange juxtaposer. She had her affair with Marinetti. As I've mentioned. And what happened then was that the gentleness, and the sharp eye, and the kind of lovely sexy anarchy of Mina Loy was conjoined with the machine-admiring bullying mechanistic destructiveness and manicness of Marinetti. And out of these two forces, Marinetti and Mina Loy, was begotten a young bully who talked loudly and sneered in public. His name was Ezra Pound. Sara Teasdale disliked Ezra Pound, and Ezra Pound disliked Sara Teasdale, so it was mutual.

And that's what I want to talk to you about. I want to clarify the sweep of it all. And the grandeur of it all. And the tragic waste of it all. The perversion of talents. The discouragement of gifts. The misapplication of energies. And even so, the flowering of some really nice poems along the way.

LITTLE INJURY TODAY, actually. I was carrying my computer downstairs in order to continue the cleanup of my office, which is progressing well, although slowly. I thought if I get my computer out of there—my big old computer, not my laptop—I'll be able to reach the next phase of cleaning. So I unhooked all the little machines that are connected to the big machine. I unhooked the power cord and the two external drives that I have, and the optical mouse with the little red eye in its belly, and the speakers, and the monitor, and the scanner, and the printer, and the keyboard, and I guess that's it. I looked at the USB cables dangling there, and I laughed pityingly at them, and I thought, Whoever designed the connector of the USB cable was a man who despised the human race, because you can't tell which way to turn it and you waste minutes of your tiny day, crouched, grunting, trying the half-blocked connector one way and the next.

So there I was. My computer was as if amputated—all of its ways of connecting to the world were gone, and it was just a black obelisk with a rich man's name on it. It couldn't reason, it couldn't speak, it was imprisoned in its frozen memories, its self was in a state of suspension. It could not add anything to what it had done, or remember anything that it had done.

I lifted it carefully and I said aloud in the room, "Man, this sucker's heavy." When you think that there are plenty of laptops for sale that do most of what this thing does. But it's still a good computer even now three years after I bought it.

So I carried it through various rooms, past various piles of books, and then I began walking down the stairs. And these stairs have something about them that makes me misjudge. Not for the first time I believed that my foot had reached the final stair when it hadn't. I thought I was stepping down onto the floor but really I had one step to go. So my foot came down twice as hard as it should have and eight inches lower than it should have, very heavily, and I was thrown forward by my out-of-balance, almost toppling, landing. I was really falling. If I dropped the computer I could catch my fall. But I didn't want to drop the computer. So I did a strange low dance of clutching the computer and running forward. I was like a mother chimp fleeing with her baby. I ran three forward-falling steps, and then my hand, holding the corner of the computer, collided with the edge of a doorjamb. I set the computer down hard. But I hadn't let it fall.

Immediately I thought I'd broken my finger, which was bleeding and had no sensation. I went into the kitchen and stood at the sink, and then I started to faint, so I went to the couch with some paper towels and lay down to bleed.

I held my hand in the air, and I kept testing my finger, wondering whether the bone in it was broken. I really didn't want to go to a doctor and have them say, Ah-hah, we'll X-ray it and give you a bone scan and a barium enema, just to be sure. No thank you. I have no health insurance. Death is my health insurance. So I lay there and breathed steadily, and after a while my finger stopped bleeding, and the feeling of mild shock passed, and my knuckle turned gray and then a bruised blue. And I knew that I was going to be fine, but that I might not be able to type for a while, which would give me a reprieve on writing my introduction. A great whimpery happiness passed through me like clear urine.

I COULDN'T THINK of who to call, so I called Roz's cellphone and told her I'd stumbled on the stairs, and she arrived amazingly quickly and pulled up a chair and took the bunched-up paper towels away and looked at my finger. She is very good at taking care of a person who has hurt his finger. She had brought some bandages, and she bandaged me up. She said, "You probably need stitches. I can take you to the hospital." I said no, no, I'll just let the skin do what skin does.

Then I said I thought I would take a nap. Roz patted my shoulder, which felt good. Then she walked Smack and left.

I lay there wondering why I had fallen. Why am I in such a rush? Why can't I just feel my way carefully down the last several steps? I've had problems with those steps before. You think the flat plane of the floor is there and your whole balance system has already compensated for the landing on the floor, and then it's not there, and you fall. It's a short fall, only eight inches, but it's a forward fall.

And what if I'd hit my head? I thought, Poor Edna. That was how Edna St. Vincent Millay died, falling down the stairs alone. She'd written that embarrassingly bad propaganda poetry during the war, and she knew her singing days were done. She was drunk, and I wasn't really. I'd just had two Newcastles. Not drunk but not in a state of tip-top balance either. It's not good to live alone when you fall down the stairs.

Vachel Lindsay died on the stairs, too, more or less. After drinking poison, Vachel Lindsay staggered up the basement stairs. His wife called, Is everything all right? He said no. And when Vachel Lindsay died Sara Teasdale was heartsick, and she drugged herself one night in the bathtub.

I fell asleep for about an hour with my bloody finger on my chest. Fortunately it was my left index finger. There were some small cuts on my right hand, but they also had stopped bleeding. I looked at the cuts for a while before I went to sleep.

WHEN I FIRST started reading the *Norton Anthology of Poetry* in college, I thought, There's a problem here. There are too many poems about death. Death, churchyards, wormy cadavers. Death is really a small part of life, and it's not the part that you want to concentrate on, because life is life and it's full of untold particulars. For example, take my briefcase. Is there anything about death in my briefcase? Let me reach in, with my good hand, and I'll feel around. Ah: a raisin. Will you look at that dusty raisin? Actually it may be a dried cranberry.

And what else? A yellow clamp to hold papers together. And a green clamp. Both useful. And a Cruzer USB Flash stick. And here's a crumpled receipt from a car-repair place that says CUSTOMER STATES THERE IS A RATTLE NOISE UNDER VEHICLE. It's been stamped P A I D in green ink with a woman's initials in red. And here's a small notebook with some passages from Dryden copied into it. And here's a bubble pack of Pilot G2 Rolling Ball pens, with two pens left in it. And, what else? A crumpled sleeve for an Amtrak ticket. And a visitor badge with my name on it, and on the back it says: "This visitor badge can be used as an adhesive badge or non-adhesive badge." And here's an untwisted twist tie. And here's a dime, and a penny, and a nickel. And a sixteen-pack of Duracell AA batteries. They say:

GREAT VALUE

GRANDE VALEUR

Six batteries left. And it turns out I've been carrying around a New York subway map and didn't know it.

And that's just one side pouch. So, anything about death

in there? No! Well, yes. The Dryden couplet in the notebook is about death. It's in what experts call iambic pentameter:

> All human things are subject to decay
> And, when Fate summons, monarchs must obey.

But spending your life concentrating on death is like watching a whole movie and thinking only about the credits that are going to roll at the end. It's a mistake of emphasis.

On the other hand, maybe my briefcase is wrong. Poems do seem to want to announce, over and over, that life's warm zephyrs are blowing past and the gravestones are just beyond the next rise. Little groupings of gravestones, all leaning and cracked, with a rusty black Victorian fence around them. They're just over that rise. Poets never want to forget that. And actually we need to hear that sometimes. And we need poems to declare love, too. Which they do, over and over. I love you, or I love her, or I love him—love is behind a huge mass of poems—and that's good. Because actually those are two truths that we should keep on thinking about for ourselves. I love you, and all the people I know and depend on are going to reach the end of their lives and when they go it's completely unexpected even when part of you knew it was in the offing.

You CAN TAKE IT a step further and say, as Herrick did, "Gather ye rosebuds." Go ahead, say it if you must. But know it's a typo. It was supposed to be "Gather your rosebuds"—the "ye" was an abbreviation for "your" but with an "e" in place of the "r." It was corrected to "your" in the second edition. So, yes, you can say enjoy the panoply now, friends, gather your rosebuds, make the best bouquet of them you can manage, use all the sprigs of baby's breath you care to use, because time is on the march and you must, of course, "seize the day."

But here's the thing. Horace didn't say that. "Carpe diem" doesn't mean seize the day—it means something gentler and more sensible. "Carpe diem" means pluck the day. Carpe, pluck. Seize the day would be "cape diem," if my school Latin serves. No R. Very different piece of advice.

What Horace had in mind was that you should gently pull on the day's stem, as if it were, say, a wildflower or an olive, holding it with all the practiced care of your thumb and the side of your finger, which knows how to not crush easily crushed things—so that the day's stalk or stem undergoes increasing tension and draws to a thinness, and a tightness, and then snaps softly away at its weakest point, perhaps leaking a little milky sap, and the flower, or the fruit, is released in your hand. Pluck the cranberry or blueberry of the day tenderly free without damaging it, is what Horace meant—pick the day, harvest the day, reap the day, mow the day, forage the day. Don't freaking grab the day in your fist like a burger at a fairground and take a big chomping bite out of it. That's not the kind of man that Horace was.

And yet if it hadn't been wrongly translated as "seize" would we remember that line now? Probably not. "Pluck the day free"? No way. And would we have remembered "gather ye rosebuds" without the odd mistake of the "ye"? Probably not. It's their wrongness that kept these ideas alive.

9

I WENT ON A BLUEBERRY-PICKING DATE with Tim and Tim's new girlfriend Hannah and Hannah's friend Marie. I kind of liked Marie. She wore flowing scarflike garments and some kind of weird perfume, and she knew a lot about Dorothy Parker. She stuck her head inside one of the taller blueberry bushes and then she said, "You know, the really good ones are deep inside."

I said, "Are they?" I stuck my head in, and Marie was right. If you push your head way into the green shadow of the bush and then you look up, you'll find amazing pendular arrangements of giant almost-black berries hanging everywhere. Nobody's seen them but you. They've been there all along, growing an ever darker blue and ever more engorged with rainwater, and yet no previous pickers have found them because they did not know to push their whole head into the blueberry bush.

"You have the gift," I said. "But I don't think you're going to develop any feelings of affection for me. Am I right?"

"Let's just pick blueberries," she said. So we picked a whole lot of blueberries, and then the four of us walked to the water and smelled its mumbling muddy smell, and Tim suddenly held out his arms and said, "Look at this river!"

I said to Marie, "Can you give us a taste of some Dorothy P?"

Marie lifted both sides of her scarf and said:

> Devil-gotten sinners,
>> Throwing back their heads,
> Fiddling for their dinners,
>> Kissing for their beds.

We all went "Oooo." Then Tim and Hannah began to walk back up toward the porch where you weighed the blueberries and left the right amount of money in a little wooden box. I made a tiny flinch of embarrassment as I saw the two of them hold hands. Marie and I walked behind them, not knowing what to do with our arms.

"So do you, ah, blame Walt Whitman for the death of rhyme?" Marie asked, conversationally.

I said, "Just because he said rhyming was intrinsically comic, that it was for inferior writers? No, that's just Walt talking out his back hatch. Which he was wont to do. Rationalizing his own inabilities. He wrote some things of genius, and he made his own rules." I paused. "What's that odd rattling sound?"

The sun was dipping behind the trees, and a frizzle of wind had risen up from somewhere. We listened. The sound turned out to be coming from several small windmills that had begun turning. We walked up to one and looked at it.

"Looks to be made out of a beer can," said Marie.

"You are right," I said. It was a Pabst beer can, cut and fanned out to make a windmill. When it twirled, it frightened berry-eating birds away. "That was a nice stanza you said back there," I said. "Some would say that it was trochaic trimeter, but they would be wrong in my opinion because it's a four-beat line."

"Oh," she said. "Glad to know that."

When we reached the car, we smiled and waved goodbye.

I TOOK A DIFFERENT EXIT on the highway because I wanted to go to Roz's place. As I drove I thought, no, it really wasn't that Whitman killed rhyme, it was that Jules Laforgue translated Whitman into French. The translating exoticized him, and then one day Laforgue wrote Gustave Kahn and said, Gustave, my frère, I forgot to rhyme. Because remember, a lot of French free verse is only sort of free. It rhymes and it scans, it just doesn't follow the superstrict rules that Boileau laid down way back in the day. But we aren't really conscious of the traditionalism of the French symbolists because French vers libre in English prose translation doesn't rhyme. The death of rhyme is really all about translation. Everybody started wanting to write poetry that sounded like a careful, loving prose version of some sweet-voiced balladeer from a faraway land. Everybody read the prose in their own language, and then they imagined the glorious versificational paradise that they didn't inhabit but that was glimmering greenly there in the distant original. The imagined rhyme-world was actually better and more lyrical than if they had the original poem in the original language with the actual rhyme scheme in it in front of them.

It happened first in French with Poe's poems. Poe was the juiciest rhymer of the nineteenth century—before Swinburne, that is—but Mallarmé in his wisdom translated Poe into exquisitely rhymeless French prose, and then Mallarmé published his reverent prose translations in a book, with line drawings by Manet. I don't own the book, because it's valuable, but I looked at it in a library once.

So then the French prose translations of Poe fed back into English poetry—and real rhyme, as opposed to imagined rhyme in a different language, began to seem somehow too obvious, too easy.

And the main thing was, it was kind of old Tim to want

me to meet Marie, but I just wasn't going to call her up and ask her out. I wasn't going to do it. For one thing, she hadn't liked me that much. Her first impression was not dazzlement, understandably. So I'd really have to huff and puff to pique her interest. And although, yes, I liked that she had written her thesis on Dorothy Parker, and although yes I thought her scarf was colorful, in a way it made no dang difference because I wanted to be in the kitchen with Roz while she picked fleas off my dog, with the dishwasher humming warmly in the background.

I THOUGHT AGAIN of standing in the field of blueberry bushes listening to the rattle of the Pabst beer can windmills. And then suddenly I remembered a certain photograph that is printed in Karl Shapiro's autobiography.

In Karl Shapiro's autobiography there's a picture of Shapiro sitting at a round table with some of his students, and one of his students is Ted Kooser. Ted Kooser is an agreeable-looking young man with sticky-outy ears, and he's sitting in front of two beers—Pabst beers. Pabst is what reminded me. One of the beers may belong to the person who is taking the photo—who may be Karl Shapiro's wife, or another student, it doesn't say—or it may be that the two beers were both drunk by Ted Kooser himself. They look that way, but I doubt very much that he's an overdoer of beer. He just doesn't strike me as one.

Karl Shapiro's poems were included in a very important anthology, *The Oxford Book of American Verse*, edited by F. O. Matthiessen. Matthiessen lived very near Portsmouth, in Kittery, Maine, with his lover, a painter. Several editions of *The Oxford Book of American Verse* came out, and each time Shapiro's poems were inside. And then F. O. Matthiessen jumped out a hotel room window in Boston, because he was lonely and sad and upset about the purge of former communists. This was the fifties and things had gotten crazy, and Matthiessen jumped.

So Oxford waited politely for some years, and then they hired a different anthologist, a man named Richard Ellman, who was big on James Joyce, to edit *The New Oxford Book of English Verse*. Ellman hated Shapiro, because for one thing Shapiro had sharply criticized the Pound-Eliot-Joyce axis, and so he, Ellman, dropped Shapiro's poems from the anthology. Just expunged him—blotted him right out. Shapiro was gone from the Oxford anthology. And he really never recovered. In his autobiography he said it was like dying.

Many years later, Ted Kooser, Shapiro's student, became poetry consultant at the Library of Congress, a.k.a. Poet Laureate of the United States. And another edition of the Oxford anthology came out. Now it's called *The Oxford Book of American Poetry*. "Verse" sounded too tea-tableish by that time. This new new version is edited by David Lehman, a poet—and guess what? Karl Shapiro is back in. So it all comes around. Ted Kooser isn't in it, and I'm not in it, but I never was, and I don't mind.

Roz wasn't there when I got to her apartment. I left a container of blueberries by her door. I put a really big smoky one on top, and a leaf.

THERE USED TO BE a position at the Library of Congress called "poetry consultant." Which isn't a very newsworthy title. The first poetry consultant was a man named Joseph Auslander. "Auslander" means outlander. And Archie MacLeish, who became Librarian of Congress in 1939, didn't think much of Auslander's poetry. So the man was gently pushed aside. And then began a long line of poetry consultants. Louise Bogan, and Elizabeth Bishop, and Léonie Adams, and others were all poetry consultants. William Carlos Williams was going to be a poetry consultant in the early fifties, and then it came out that he had a taint of communism in his past—suddenly William Carlos Williams couldn't be the consultant.

Then, many years after that, sometime in the eighties, the library did a brilliant thing. And I don't know whose idea it was. Maybe it was Daniel Boorstin's idea. Maybe it was Billy Collins's idea. I don't know. I don't know anything really about Billy Collins except that he's Mister Bestseller. Maybe it was Robert Penn Warren's idea.

But they thought, Let's get these people in but let's give them the old fancy title, the honorary title that Tennyson had. Let's call them "poet laureates." What does "poet laureate" mean? Nothing. It means a person with laurel branches twined around his head. Which is not something people do much now. A little headdress of leaves, a little fancy, leafy hat. Nobody does that now. But even so we're going to copy the English model, and we're going to say, Okay, Tennyson was the poet laureate, and after him there was somebody, was it Bridges? Somebody innocuous. We're going to have these people come, and the publicists are going to go wild and they're going to say Billy Collins, Poet Laureate. And before that Robert Pinsky, Poet Laureate. Maybe it was Pinsky's idea. He's a pretty smooth dude. He used to be the poetry editor of *The New Republic*. Rejected some things of mine and more power to him.

And then in time it became retroactive. So the publicists would say that such-and-such poetry consultant—Louise Bogan, maybe, or Elizabeth Bishop—were the poet laureates of their time. "A position now known," the press kit would say, "as Poet Laureate of the United States." Even a guy like William Stafford was the poetry consultant. It was very different from the English model, because there were term limits. You were only poet laureate for a few years, not for your lifetime. Very different indeed from the English way, in which you were appointed like a Supreme Court Justice and served till you went gaga, or died.

Now, John Dryden was an early poet laureate of England. Dryden is one of those poets who wrote many thousands of lines of poetry and left very little of himself behind. His biographers have a hard time figuring out what he was up to in any given year. He lived through revolution, restoration, plague, and fire, and all we have is his published writing and a few letters to go on. But it's enough. It's all you need. Dryden defended rhyme against Milton, who said it was barbarous. He was funny, he was easy, he was a great prose writer and a great rhymer. This is unusual, in that most good poets can't write good prose. The better the prose they write, the worse the poetry. The better the poetry, the worse the prose. Except for letters. Poets are good letter writers. Elizabeth Bishop wrote absolute killer letters. Louise Bogan wrote killer letters, too, and funny, jabbing reviews. Those two sit way over here in the twentieth century. Whereas Dryden is over here in the seventeenth century. He was a short man. Elizabeth Bishop was a short woman.

Louise Bogan was a tall woman. She read in a very formal manner, with an exaggeratedly correct upper-class accent. She says, "This, is Louise Bogan, and I'm going to read a poem called—" whatever. And then she reads it slowly, with great pauses. And it's very very compressed, and that's what I like about it, it's packed, it's like a shoe in a shoe tree. A Ted Roethke poem is like an empty shoe you find at the side of the road that some manic person has cast aside on a walk, but Louise Bogan's poems are like cared-for shoes in a closet, tight and heavy around their clacking wooden trees.

TODAY THE CLOUDS have been sprayed on the sky with a number 63 narrow-gauge titanium sprayer tip. I don't want to sit in the barn just now, so I'm sitting out near the "thorny brambles," as I call them. I know very little about them except that they grow and grow and that they cover the hillside now, and when I pass by them with my lawnmower buzzing they catch at my shirt and my arm with their remarkably hooklike sharp thorns. Roz says they're a species of rose.

I've done nothing all week. Had a call from Victor and talked more about the reading series. Measured Nan's room. Drove to Portland listening to a CD of Elizabeth Bishop reading "The Fish." Cried, beating the steering wheel, because she was so good and she sounded so young. Booped the horn by mistake. Apologized with hand gestures to people around me on Route 95. Toured the Longfellow house in Portland while a group of kids from poetry camp chanted, in unison, "I shot an arrow into the air." Thought I saw John Greenleaf Whittier lurking in the shadows of the dark Longfellow kitchen, studying the gnarled blue tree in a large china tureen. Nodded at him. Opened a very unpleasant bill on my return. Ate a sandwich at a café with a nice short woman I met at the video store. Threw out my jaw because the bread was so crusty. Agreed to review two books to raise money:

one a book of the art of Boris Artzybasheff, a surrealist illus-
trator who painted a lot of covers for *Time*, and one an interesting book about steam trains and poetry in the nineteenth
century. Am I becoming a critic? Fine, I don't mind.

Then yesterday, another minor adventure in self-
mutilation. I'd bought a big round loaf of bread from the
bakery, and I cut off the nub end of it, and I did not put
butter on it. I have something quite remarkable to tell
you about butter, but maybe that's for another time. Oh,
might as well tell you now. Unsalted butter is flavored. For
instance, I buy unsalted Land O' Lakes butter—but this
observation applies to all major brands of butter—and I
didn't realize this until Roz pointed it out a few years ago.
Roz has very keen tastebuds. All unsalted butter has so
called "natural" flavoring. Real butter is flavored with butter flavor. Just think about that. I didn't believe it till I read
the ingredients. Butter-flavored butter. When you know
that fact, you'll taste it and it'll drive you nuts. How long
has this outrage been going on?

So I had a slice of bread, and a few calamata olives, and
I started singing "Saved by a woman," by Ray LaMontagne,
at the top of my lungs, while cutting a second slice, and I got
a little jiggy with the bread knife, which is new and sharp
with squared-off serrations, and I cut off a small dome of my
fingermeat. It was very similar to cutting off the end of the
loaf of bread, except that it hurt. I said some bad words and
bled on the bread, and then I went upstairs to the bathroom

and did my best to reposition the sliced-off part where it was supposed to go, and although the blood continued I was able to encircle the fingertip—my left hand's index fingertip—with two Band-Aids. It was the same finger that had crashed into the doorjamb, if you can believe it. I didn't call Roz because two cuts on the same finger is an embarrassment, and I've gotten quite good at self-Band-Aiding. I hope the skin is going to graft itself back on. I lay on my bed and stared at the ceiling, worrying about my credit-card debt and eating calamata olives. And now it's Thursday.

THURSDAY IS THE DAY of fear. On Monday you're in great shape because you've got the whole week. Then Tuesday, still pretty good, still at the beginning more or less. Then Wednesday, and you're poised, and you can accomplish much if you just apply yourself vigorously and catch up. And then suddenly, you're driving under that huge tattered banner, with that T and that H and that U and that frightening R and the appalling S—THURSDAY—and you slide down the steep slope toward the clacking shredder blades that wait on Sunday afternoon. Another whole week of your one life. Your one "precious life," as Mary Oliver says. You don't have too many Thursdays left. There are after all only fifty-two of them in the year. Fifty-two may sound like a lot, but when Thursdays come around, fifty-two doesn't seem like a lot at all. I just wish I had more money.

Karl Shapiro taught. Ted Roethke taught. Money is a problem. I think I'm going to have to start teaching again.

No, no, no, no, no. I can't. I can't teach. It killed me. Those nice kids stunned my brain. I'll never recover from that year. I can't do it again. Any fate is preferable. It was death on toast.

The first week I told them to memorize a couple of poems, and I said, Here's what a poem is. See this glass of water? This glass of water is an essay. Perfectly fine thing for it to be. A literary essay—a piece of "creative nonfiction." But dip a spoon in that glass of water and scoop some of it out and hold it over a hot fry pan so that a few drops fall and sizzle and quickly disappear. That's a poem. And they nodded. They got it. And while they nodded I remembered when my mother would lick her finger and then touch the iron and I'd smell the tiny innocent smell of her fried spit. I remembered how I really liked that smell. But I didn't tell them that. Because there are limits to what you can tell students. I just made a little drumroll on the table with my fists, and I said, So guys, I want you to get some poems by heart and I want you to rhyme me up some nice little sizzlers.

And they tried. They were eager kids. They worked at it. But they weren't rhymers. And this is what everyone who teaches poetry discovers. If you ask grade-school kids to rhyme, it may sound jingly, but it's an appealingly artless jingle. If you ask college kids to rhyme, however, they're going to sound awful. Because the percentage of genuine rhymers is tiny. If you ask them to write a poem that doesn't rhyme, on the other hand, it's not so clear that they lack the basal gift. They may come up with something that has a rawness and a quick quiet stab of honesty and even wit sometimes—if you don't ask them to rhyme. And so there you are, a person who has loved rhyme all your life, and what are you saying to the impressionable people you are teaching? You're saying, *And remember—it doesn't have to rhyme.*

So I learned that lesson first, and it was a painful one. But there was a larger unhappiness, too—a darker kind of knowledge that sprouted and blossomed and uncoiled its thorns in me over the semester. Which was that I was being paid to lie. My job was to lie very gently to these trusting, sleepy, easily wounded students, over and over again, by saying in all sorts of different ways that their poems were interesting and powerful and sharply etched and nicely turned and worth giving collective thought to. Which they were unfortunately not. One student wrote some good poems. And maybe she would go on to something, who knows? But most of them—no way. I remember one of her poems used the phrase "his goldfish hair."

So I was a professional teller of lies. And if I kept teaching, I would be telling more and more lies to more and more of these students, year after year. Soon they and their poems would merge. I pictured one of those pale inhuman computer-generated faces that you get if you superimpose a thousand real faces. All the individual voices in all of their individual poems would blend into one ghostly student megapoem—and it would float there, hovering, staring at me, waiting for me to tell it that it was good work. And I knew what the very first word of the megapoem would be. The first word would be: "I."

I. Now "I" is a really good word. It's a useful word. For instance, Elizabeth Bishop starts off "The Fish" with "I." "I caught a tremendous fish." And I've begun many a poem with "I." Because you've got to. And what I understood was that my own dear students were destroying "I" for me. Which is another way of saying that they were destroying me.

So I QUIT. I did it in the second month of the spring semester, on a Thursday. There was a new batch of students around the table. Same overbright classroom, same malevolent chairs. The one good poet had gone off to Taiwan, and I missed her faint perfume of promise. They all handed their week's work in, and I lifted the pile of fresh poems in the air to feel its weight. It was unusually heavy, because one of the poems was twenty pages long. I knew who it was by. It was called "Pythagoras Unbound," and it was by an overeager boy who talked a lot about Czeslaw Milosz. I skimmed the first page and I saw the word "endoplasm" and I went cold, like I'd eaten a huge plate of calamari. As the hour was ending, I said, "Folks, just a heads-up. I want you to know that I won't be able to read some of the poetry that you've just given me. I will be writing a 'U.R.' on some of your poems.

What does U.R. mean? It means 'Un Read.' I will want very much to read every word of all your poems, because my duty as your instructor is to read them, but in some cases I will not be able to, because, I'm sorry, I can't. And so for some of you the grade that I give you will be based from here on entirely on class participation. Or if you're silent and shy and thoughtful and don't talk at all in class, that's all right, I fully respect that, I'll just grade you on those sudden gleams of thoughtful insight that I detect in your eyes. An alert look in your eyes is probably more predictive of your future success than any poetry you will write any time soon."

The students listened with hurt puzzlement. They didn't like the U.R. idea. They wanted me to read their poems. Who else would read them? And when else in their lives would they be so alive and so full of the wish to do something new and good? I realized I'd gone too far. "I'm just joshing," I said. "I'm looking forward to this new work. Thanks for it. Have a great weekend."

After that class I went to the dean and told her I wasn't coming back in September. And that was the end of my teaching career.

ELIZABETH BISHOP was a short woman. She wanted to be taller. She had amazing up-floofing hair with a streak of white. And she didn't like the idea of teaching creative writing. She wrote May Swenson: "I think one of the worst things I know about modern education is this 'Creative Writing' business." But she did it anyway. She didn't want to be a drunk, but she was. Sometimes, she said, she drank like a fish. Lota, her Brazilian lover, wanted her to take antabuse and she didn't want to, and she left Brazil. Then Lota went into a gloom and killed herself.

Today I was punching down the garbage with my fist in the tall kitchen can, to make more room before I had to take it out to the barn—going, Yah, yah, punch it down!—and my right thumb caught on the wavy edge of the lid of a tunafish can and I sliced it. Not too badly. Not off. I rinsed the cut in the sink, and I thought, What's with all these minor finger injuries? What's happening to me? I'm wearing three Band-Aids now. I'm a three Band-Aid man.

Everyone always wanted Elizabeth Bishop to read aloud "The Fish," because it's good, and she grew to hate it and to dread reading it. She wrote to Robert Lowell that she was thinking of rewriting it as a sonnet. Its prosiness made her unhappy. She'd moved on and forgotten why the poem is so good.

The poem is in this book here. Look at this paperback. Just white and yellow and blue, simple as can be. Elizabeth Bishop's *The Complete Poems*. Don't look at my Band-Aids, just look at the book. It's a Farrar, Straus and Giroux book and they always, in this era, had the most beautiful cover designs. Six dollars and ninety-five cents is what it cost me. Bob Giroux was her editor.

And here is the original bookmark, from the bookstore where I bought the book. The Grolier book shop in Cambridge. Little poetry shop on a side street off Harvard Square. It's had some tough times recently.

"The Fish" takes up three pages. It's long. It starts here, and it goes over here, and then it goes over to here. And every word on these three pages is worth reading. In her letter to I think it's Marianne Moore, she says that she feels very adventurous because she's not capitalizing the first letter of each line.

The way to read the poem is not to read it in the book, but to listen to her read it on a CD. She has a such a marvelously simple way of delivering it. She just seems to shrug it off her. It's of no interest to her that it's poetry. There's no fancy emphasis. It's almost flat, the way she reports it, and she has a slight midwesternness to her voice. It's so lovely, and she sounds very young and surprised that she's been asked to read it.

You know what "The Fish" is? "The Fish" is sort of like a Talk of the Town piece in *The New Yorker* if the Talk of the Town had died and gone to heaven. That's what it is, a perfect Talk of the Town piece. Except that it doesn't use the "we." And it didn't appear in *The New Yorker*—it appeared in *Partisan Review.* And I don't even care whether it's called a poem or not. It doesn't scan. She was a woman who was very capable of rhyming. Who liked rhyming. But this one is not a rhyming poem.

The Fish! The fish. "I caught a tremendous fish." Here's the situation. Elizabeth Bishop is in a boat, on her own, it seems, and she's caught a tremendous fish, that's come out of the ocean. What does the fish want to do? The fish wants to get back to the water. But she doesn't let it. She examines it very closely. She looks at its peeling skin and compares it to old wallpaper. She repeats the word "wallpaper" twice in two lines of a poem—an unheard-of prosiness. And then she bends closer, and she looks right into the fish's eye. She says it's larger than her eye but shallower. And that's true—we all know those shallow fish eyes. "The irises backed and packed / with tarnished tinfoil." She's really peering at that fish's eye now. And then, whoa: the eye shifts. The fish eye moves. Terror. We know right then for sure that it's alive.

All that careful slow description suddenly has a kind of near panic in it, because we know that the fish is out of its element, breathing in the terrible oxygen. The fish doesn't want to be described. That's what gives the poem its pull. The fish resists description because it just wants to be back in the water, and not to be seen, but she's insisting on looking at it and coming up with one simile after another. All these wonderful similes take time, and meanwhile the fish is start-ing to suffocate.

So we look at his skin, at his scales, at his swim bladder, which is like a peony, and his eyes. And then, we get to "the mechanism of his jaw." And here's where we learn about the fish's history—the five pieces of broken-off fishing line. And she describes each kind of fishing line. One line is green, and the others are black, and we hear all about them. And those lines are allegorical. They're lines of what? Of poetry. Because we know that other people—other anglers, other hopeful poets—have caught this very same ancient, real fish. Their lines are there, hooked into the fish's jaw, all the many other attempts to rhyme this old fish into poetry. Rupert Brooke has a beautiful poem about this very same fish. But Elizabeth Bishop's hooked it now, and she's *not* going to rhyme it, she's just going to tell us about it.

And that's what leads her to her last line, when she's there in the boat, and the fish is gasping and—ploosh—"I let the fish go." Because that's what you have to do. You take the moment, you do your best to describe it, it fascinates you, and then when you've done your best to give it to people on some printed page, then you have to let it go.

For the rest of her life, when she was asked to give a reading, they wanted her to read that poem. Till she completely lost track of the reality behind it and didn't want anything to do with it and wished the anthologists would pick something else.

And if you listen to her reading it, you'll notice that there's a tiny moment just after she says "And I let the fish go" before the tape hiss stops. In these old poetry recordings, the audio engineer always pulled the level down too soon, immediately after the last word, without any mental reverb time, and oddly enough it works beautifully. You hear "Ffff, and I let the the fish go, ffff—" and then silence. You're in the empty blankness before the next poem. The black water. The fish is already gone, out of hearing. Even the hiss of the tape, the water in which the fish swam, is gone. You have to return reality to itself after you've struggled to make a poem out of it. Otherwise it's going to die. It needs to breathe in its own world and not be examined too long. She knew that. The fish slips away unrhymed.

I think I'm going to go to RiverRun Books and look at the poetry shelves. When I see new books for sale there that I already own, it makes me happy. It makes me feel that there's part of the world that I really understand.

10

Thomas Edison's people convinced Alfred Tennyson to chant the "Charge of the Light Brigade" into a microphone. You can hear it in a BBC collection, and you can hear it in a CD that comes with a book called *The Voice of the Poet*. Tennyson sounds like this:

> pkkkfffffffrrrfffff-fff! pkkkfffffffrrrfffff-fff!
> pkkkfffffffrrrfffff-fff! pkkkfffffffrrrfffff-fff!
> Hobble leg, hobble leg,
> hobble leg owhmmm!
> Into the bottle of fluff, rubbed the stuff under!

pkkkffffffrrrffff-fff! pkkkffffffrrrffff-fff!
pkkkffffffrrrffff-fff! pkkkffffffrrrffff-fff!

But under the static of the wax cylinder, did you hear what Lord Alfred was up to? He was using the regular four-beat line, but he was using triplets within each beat. One-two-three, one-two-three:

① ② ③ ② ② ③ ③ ② ③ ④ ② ③
Half a league, **half** a league, **half** a league **on**ward
① ② ③ ② ② ③ ③ ② ③ ④ ② ③
All in the **vall**ey of Death, **rode** the six **hun**dred.

That's how he reads it, with the triplets. Triplets are called dactyls or anapests in the official lingo, depending on whether they start with an upbeat or not. But those words are bits of twisted dead scholarship, and you should forget them immediately. Put them right out of your head. Wave them away. The poetry here is made up of triplets.

Triplets are good for all kinds of emotions. People think they're funny—and they are. They work in light verse and in limericks. "There was a young man from North Feany—rest. Who sprinkled some gin on his weenie—rest." Dr. Seuss uses them: "A yawn is quite catching, you see, like a cough." Ya-ta-ta, ta-ta-ta, ta-ta-ta, tum. Light.

Or you can use them for a love scene:

① ② ③ ② ② ③ ③ ② ③ ④ ②
She **turns** her face **toward** you, her **large** eyes up**lift**ed
③① ② ③ ② ② ③ ③ ② ③ ④
Di**la**ted, and **dark,** with a **pass**ionate **fire;**
② ③ ① ② ③ ② ② ③ ③ ② ③ ④ ②
And her **rich,** dewy **lips** in their **in**nocent **fond**ness,
③ ① ② ③ ② ② ③ ③ ② ③ ④
Fill **up** in full **mea**sure your **cup** of de**sire.**

That's by Mary Louise Ritter, a forgotten poet, out of an old anthology called *Everybody's Book of Short Poems,* which once sold thousands of copies.

Or you can use triplets to dispense advice:

① ② ③ ② ② ③ ③ ② ③ ④② ③
One **can**not make **bar**gains for **bliss**es   **(rest)**
Or catch them like fishes in nets   (rest)
And sometimes the things that life misses   (rest)
Help more than the things that it gets.   (rest)

That's a poem by Alice Carey that was very big a century ago. If you read it aloud, you might feel yourself declaiming it too bouncily. But if you sing it, you'll find that you slow down and you begin to hear the wisdom in what she's saying:

James Fenton—who is the best living love poet—uses this same triplet rhythm, with the same end-rest on a four-beat line and the same warningness: "It's something you say at your peril (rest) / It's something you shouldn't contain (rest)."

And you can mix triplets together with duplets. Swinburne was the great rhythmic mixmaster, and before him Christina Rossetti. And Vachel Lindsay was good at it, too. Vachel Lindsay was a chanter and drumbeater. In the twenties, for a short time, he was probably the most famous poet in the U.S.A. Listen to what he does.

Factory **win**dows are **al**ways **bro**ken.
Something or other is going wrong.
Something is rotten—I think, in Denmark.
End of factory-window song.

Now what has he got going there? He's got triplets in the first part of the line—"factory windows are"—and doublets in the second part—"always broken."

154

Bumpada, bumpada, bumpum, bumpum
Bumpada, bumpada, bumpum, bumpum
Factory windows are always broken
Diddle a diddle America
We want to live in America.

It's everywhere.

And sometimes the rhythm isn't a double or a triple, it's a quadruple rhythm. In other words, sixteenth notes, not eighth notes. And sometimes, often in fact, it's a quadruple rhythm made up of an eighth note plus two sixteenth notes that lead you into the next eighth note. That sounds complicated, but when you hear it you'll recognize it as obvious and familiar—something you've been listening to for your whole life. "Death comes with a crawl, or he comes with a pounce," as Edmund Vance Cooke said.

I'm dancing around the barn with my new broom. Dum deem, deedledeem, deedledeem, deedledeem!

———————

WHEN I WAS IN COLLEGE nobody mentioned Vachel Lindsay. Not even a whisper of his name. I heard a lot about Pound and Eliot. We had to read "Prufrock," which is a lovely poem, and "The Waste Land," which is a hodge-podge of glummery and borrowed paste. And I heard about the *Spoon River Anthology,* and the Black Mountain poets, and Ginsberg and Ferlinghetti, of course, and Sylvia Plath and Ted Hughes, and end of story.

But Vachel Lindsay, in his day, was big. He went around doing a kind of vaudeville act using poetry. A one-man minstrel show. He was famous for it.

And one day on one of his tours he came to St. Louis, and there he met Sara Teasdale.

Sara Teasdale was a much better poet than Vachel Lindsay was, and he recognized that, and he fell in love with her and chanted his poems to her and beat his drum for her, and later he dedicated a book to her. And eventually he proposed to her.

She didn't marry him, because basically she saw that he was a lunatic. Very unstable and he had seizures from time to time. But they corresponded for years. And as his fame dimmed and people forgot about him, he got crazier, and he began to threaten his wife—he'd married a young teacher—and he began to have paranoid thoughts that her father was after him. His wife became terrified of him. They had very little money. And when he would go onstage at some provincial women's club, they always wanted him to do his old stuff. "Do the stuff where you bang the drum and sing about Bryant and the Big Black Bucks. Not the new stuff. We don't want the new stuff." And one night back at home he had a fit of rage, and then he calmed down and went down to the basement. His wife called down, "Are you all right, darling?" And he said, "Yes, honey, I'm quite well, thank you—I'll be up shortly."

And then in a little while she heard a sound, *blump*. And she sat up: something is not right. She rushed downstairs and there was Vachel staggering up from the basement, going *erp orp erp*. Obviously in extremis. And she said, "Darling, what's happening?"

And he said, "I drank a bottle of Lysol."

Seriously. He died of it, in agony. And it was good that he died because he could feel that he was getting violent. His time was over. He had contributed what he had to contribute. He could sense that. His kind of poetry, which was so performable and so immediately graspable, had fallen out of favor. People like Ezra Pound—who was even crazier than Vachel Lindsay was, and who also, by the way, beat a drum sometimes when he gave readings—were laughing at him. They thought he was a joke. Modernism was winning its battle with rhyme, and he didn't want to be around when Pound and Williams did their victory dance. So he left the scene.

WELL, WHEN SARA TEASDALE found out that Vachel Lindsay had died, she was unhappy, as you can imagine, because in some ways she'd always loved him. She was one of those love-at-a-distance kind of people. She'd loved several men at a distance. And women, too. His death hit her hard, and she was not a healthy woman—she was very very touchy and moody, and sensitive, and hypochondriacal, and a really fine practitioner of the four-beat line.

> O shaken flowers, o shimmering trees,
> O sunlit white and blue,
> Wound me, that I, through endless sleep,
> May bear the scar of you.

But she also wrote dirty limericks and then destroyed them. People who read them said they were some of the most incredible dirty limericks they'd ever encountered. Why, why, why did she destroy them? Why? I can hardly bear to think of this loss. Sometimes she suffered from what she called *"imeros"*—a word from Sappho that meant a kind of almost sexual craving for romance. A lust for love.

One day she hit her head on the ceiling of a taxi while it was driving over a pothole in New York, and afterward she said her brain hurt and she dropped into a funk and eventually she took morphine in the bath and died. And not long after that her friend Orrick Johns—who was also from St. Louis and also a poet, who wrote about the whiteness of plum blossoms at night—he killed himself, too. And later Edna St. Vincent Millay fell down the stairs. So the rhymers all began dying out. All except for Robert Frost. Two vast and trunkless legs of Robert Frost stood in the desert.

I'M NOT A NATURAL RHYMER. This is the great disappointment of my life. I've got a decent metrical ear—let me just say that right out—and some of my early dirty love poems rhymed because I still believed then that I could force them to, and some of those poems were anthologized in a few places. So I got a reputation as a bad-boy formalist. But these days when I try to write rhyming poetry it's terrible. I mean it's just really embarrassing—it sucks. So I write plums. Chopped garbage. I've gotten away with it for years. And I sometimes feel that maybe if I'd been born in a different time—say, 1883—and hadn't been taught haiku and free verse but real poetry, my own rhyming self would have flowered more fully.

But you know, probably not. Probably my brain just isn't arranged properly. Because think: right now we're in a time in which rhyming is going on constantly. All the rhyming in pop music. There's a lust for it. Kids have hundreds of lines of four-stress verses memorized, they just don't call it four-stress verse. They call it "the words to the songs." They call it Coldplay or Green Day or Rickie Lee Jones or the Red Hot Chili Peppers. "Now in the morning I sleep alone, /

Sweep the streets I used to own," says Coldplay. "California rest in peace / Simultaneous release," say the Red Hot Chili Peppers. Four-beat lines. Sometimes the rhymes are trite and sometimes not, and it doesn't matter because the music is the main thing. And I'm sure there will be a geniune adept who strides into our midst in five or ten years. The way Frost did. Sat up in the middle of that spring pool, with the weeds and the bugs all over him. He found the water that nobody knew was there. And that will happen again. All the dry rivulets will flow, and everyone will understand that new things were possible all along. And we'll forget almost all of the unrhymers that have been so big a part of the last fifty years. We'll forget about the wacky Charles Olson, for instance, who was once so big. My poems will definitely be forgotten. They are forgettable. They're simply not memorable. Except maybe for one or two. Maybe people will remember part of "How I Keep from Laughing." People seem to remember that one, sometimes. Garrison Keillor read it on the radio once.

NEVER MIND THAT. I soaked my skin graft in saltwater, which wasn't a good idea, but now it's healing nicely. And here's what amazes me. Howard Moss was writing poems at the same time that Allen Ginsberg was. They're so different. Sometimes it's very hard to recapture simultaneity—

because even to the people living at the time it didn't feel simultaneous. At the time it felt as if Ginsberg was over here, going "first thought best thought, first thought best thought," and Howard Moss was over here, quietly watching the sun go down through his ice cubes after a day at the office writing a letter accepting a poem sent in by Elizabeth Bishop.

Ginsberg had a poem in *The New Yorker*, too. In the sixties, Moss accepted one of Ginsberg's poems. It's a good one, too. Very long. It spreads out over parts of two pages. It begins ambitiously: "When I Die." Ginsberg's father, Louis Ginsberg, also had poems in *The New Yorker*. His poems rhymed and scanned in the old-fashioned way. But his son Allen was smitten by Walt Whitman's preacherly ampersands and he never recovered.

And one day Ginsberg was giving a talk at the Naropa Institute, where he taught, and somebody asked him what the real rhythm of his poetry was. He was in the middle of saying how bad it was for children to be taught traditional meters—the kind his father used—how the bad iambic rhythm warped their little pure Buddha minds. And somebody at the Naropa Institute said, Well then, tell us, Allen. What is the real rhythm of poetry? And Ginsberg replied that the rhythm of poetry was the rhythm of the body. He said that it was, quote, "jacking off under bridges."

And everyone went, Oh ho, chortle, provocative, ho.

Because Ginsberg's referring to jacking off under bridges and that's humorous. And it is, frankly. In fact I really like that Ginsberg would say that. It's the kind of refreshing thing that only he and some of the Beats were able to say.

So yes. Except that it isn't true. Because—try it. Just try to imagine standing under a bridge somewhere, holding a copy of *Howl*. Paperback copy.

You're under a bridge and you're holding your copy of *Howl*, and you read: "I saw the best minds of my generation zonked out on angry Koolaid in the junky slums of West 83rd street, dah dah dah dah dah dah dah dah—" Help! You can't get anywhere with that. Nobody can.

THE REAL RHYTHM of poetry is a strolling rhythm. Or a dancing rhythm. A gavotte, a minuet, a waltz. Remember those inner quadruplets I mentioned? When each beat is divided into four little pulses? Sixteenth notes, they're called, in music. Not duplets, not triplets, but quadruplets. Tetra-syllables. Some meter people call this the paeonic foot, after Aristotle. There's a useless term for you. But listen to the way they can sound:

Love has gone and left me and I don't know what to do

That's Edna St. Vincent Millay. Still four beats, but each beat has four inner fuzz-bursts of phonemic energy.

①   ②   ③   ④   ②   ②   ③ ④   ③   ②   ③   ④ ④

Love has gone and **left** me and I **don't** know what to **do**.
This or that or what you will is all the same to me
But all the things that I begin I leave before I'm through
There's little use in anything as far as I can see.

Sara Teasdale did quadruplets, too:

① ② ③ ④ ②   ②   ③ ④   ③   ② ③ ④   ④   ②   ③   ④

Let it be for**got**ten, as a **flow**er is for**got**ten

Hear it? People always say that this quadruplet rhythm is for light verse. It doesn't have to be, but it can be. Listen to this four-beater.

①   ② ③   ④ ②   ② ③ ④   ③   ② ③ ④   ④

If you **stick** a stock of **liq**uor in your **lock**er,   (rest)
It is slick to stick a lock upon your stock   (rest)
Or some joker who is slicker's going to trick you of your liquor
Though you snicker you'll feel sicker from the shock. BOOM!

That's light verse by Mr. Newman Levy. One of the lesser Algonquinites. Wrote a number of poems about alcohol, as befits a poet of the Prohibition, using that same quadruplet rhythm. Notice there's no rest on the third line, just as in a traditional ballad. W. S. Gilbert, of Gilbert and Sullivan fame, also uses it—"He's a modern major-general." And A. A. Milne:

> When the War is over and the sword at last we sheathe,
> I'm going to keep a jelly-fish and listen to it breathe.

And Thomas Bailey Aldrich: "And the heavy-branched banana never yields its creamy fruit." Vachel Lindsay used it: "Where is McKinley, that respectable McKinley"—hear the sixteenth notes in "respectable McKinley"? T. S. Eliot used it, under Vachel Lindsay's influence. "Macavity Macavity there's no one like Macavity." Rappers use it a lot—

  ①   ② ③ ④ ② ② ③   ④   ③ ②   ③ ④ ④

Shake your money **ma**ker like some**bod**y's 'bout to **pay** ya
Don't worry about them haters keep your nose up in the air

That's by Ludacris. And Kipling used it a lot, and Poe used it, too. Poe's "Raven," which is probably the best quadruplet rhythm ever written—listen to it slowly:

> And the silken, sad, uncertain rustling of each purple curtain

Isn't that smooth?

  ① ② ③   ④ ② ②   ③ ④ ③ ②   ③ ④ ④

And the **sil**ken, sad, un**cer**tain rustling **of** each purple **cur**tain
Thrilled me—filled me with fantastic terrors never felt before.

Four very slow striding beats, with four steady silken swells filling each one. It's so simple and so hypnotic.

And the metrists don't know what to do with it. Here's what one introduction to poetry says. A good introduction by John Frederick Nims. He says that Poe's "Raven" is written in—ready?—"trochaic octameter with lines two and four catalectic." Catalectic meaning cut short. And how far does that get you? It actually disables any understanding of the poem to say that what he's doing is trochaic octameter. Because it's still really a basic four-beat stanza. Poe chose to set it in a different way because the lines came out long, but it's just a ballad. He said so himself. Poe is just taking a certain kind of beautiful stroll. Whether or not he stops under a bridge is not for us to say.

I WENT TO A BEAD STORE in town, and I bought some wire and a clasp and a clamping tool. I've decided to make some of the raw beads I bought for Roz into a real string of beads and give them to her. Not as an aggressive gift, but just as a friendly gift, to thank her for helping me when my finger was bleeding. I've learned to type without using my finger, by the way. Sometimes I type "dinger" for "finger" and "invlude" for "include."

So I went to the bead store in town—Beadle Bailey, it's called. It was very quiet inside. There were thousands of beads in tiny plastic cells, and I was amazed by the choices, the profusion of possibilities. It was like being a poet in that you had indivisible units that you could string together in certain rhythms. You can't alter the nature of a given bead, or a given word, but you can change which bead you choose, and the order in which you string them on their line. And I wanted to string together the beads I chose as a gift, which meant I had a certain person in mind when I looked at the colors. I was looking at the colors with Roz's color sense in my eyeballs. And I had an ideal in mind of rhythm and of randomness. Other beaders were bending, staring into the containers, or looking at the strings of beads hanging from metal hooks on the wall.

I saw some dusty pale small ceramic beads, and I felt the immediate clench of knowing that these were the ones that Roz would like best mixed with the ones I already had from Second Avenue. I asked the beadseller at the register about clasps, and it turns out that you can buy a certain kind of magnetic clasp that frees you from the problem of fitting tiny spring-loaded hooks together. The beadseller put on her reading glasses—she had them on a black-and-yellow beaded string—and she said, "I love these," pointing to one of my selections. She put the singles in a little plastic bag, and the strings, too. The whole purchase went into a pale green paper bag, and I walked out blinking onto the street carrying the raw materials for my present to Roz and feeling a joy of knowing that I was going to make something for her—something like a poem, but better than any poem I could write.

I think I'll do a quadruplet rhythm, a love-has-gone-and-left-me rhythm: one gray-green bead and then three other beads of near-random colors, and then a gray-green bead again.

11

I LOOKED FOR AN HOUR for a certain file in my office and
couldn't find it. I found many things that I should have
acted on a long time ago and have not. I found nice letters—
unanswered letters, which cause searing guilt beyond all
imagining. Also bound galleys of books of poetry from editors hoping for a blurb. Unread and unacknowledged. These
bring less guilt, but some, because how hard would it have
been to write the editor and explain?

I didn't find the file I was looking for, which holds the
drafts of my flying spoon poems. These have swerved in and
out of my life for so many years now that I have quite a fat file.
The file now stands for the reality. I thought, If I don't find this

spoon file I won't be able to write the poem that I was put on this earth to write and my life will have been in vain.

I sprawled in bed grieving for the loss of this file, although I knew it wasn't lost but was somewhere in my office. And then I saw that the only chance I had of writing a half-decent spoon poem was in not finding the file. As soon as I had the file in hand it would smother any new upwellings I might have. I felt released from a heavy burden and I lay in bed blinking at my good fortune. Then my eye moved in a great arc across the ceiling and down the wall across the room. I saw a pile of books that I'd forgotten about, stacked leaningly under a table next to a bookcase. At the bottom of this pile was a folder about an inch thick. I knew from the familiar position of the blue Post-it notes projecting from it that it was the spoon file.

I drove to the John Greenleaf Whittier house in Haverhill, Massachusetts, and joined the tour.

WHITTIER WAS A NINETEENTH-CENTURY POET who wrote a once-famous four-beater about a blizzard, called "Snow-Bound."

On the tour, I sat down in a rocking chair that Whittier sat in. I saw the minuscule stock of books he had in the house when he was a boy, and the poem he wrote about them. It was the tour guide's last day, and she gave our little group—a family of three, a silent woman, and me—her best shot. She brought out the funny bits and the sad bits and showed us the china and the linen and told us about the yarn weasel in the guest room. You crank this weasel to measure out how much yarn you've spun—it keeps track by counting the number of clicks it makes, one click for a certain number of crankings. Hence "Pop Goes the Weasel," a poem with interesting nineteenth-century off-rhymes—"needle," "weasel"—and a surprising number of verses, because you recited it while cranking, and I guess there was a lot of yarn to measure.

Most of Whittier's poetry wasn't good, the tour guide told us. It was tedious, often, and there was too much of it. But his life was good. He'd spent eighteen years writing and editing antislavery newspapers. Once the office of a newspaper in Philadelphia was stormed by a proslavery mob. Whittier, who was the editor of the paper, stole away and put on a wig and a different outfit and joined the looters in the building. They reached his office, calling, Where's Whittier? Where's that whoreson slimedog Whittier? He broke into his office with them and was able to loot his own papers to safety before they set fire to the building. It was after the Civil War that he wrote "Snow-Bound." Which is extremely long, but has several good moments.

The tour guide almost got tearful at the end of the tour, while she sold me a postcard of the room we stood in. Her Ford Mustang was for sale, parked on the grass. She was going west to work for the State of Kentucky.

I DROVE HOME from the Whittier house, and as I drove I
thought about Whittier versus Longfellow. The two American G-rated graybeards. Longfellow was the greater poet, of
course. A strange sad man who lost two wives and a child. He
wrote a good poem called "The Day Is Done." Here's its first
stanza. I came up with a tune for it:

Hear those mixed rhythms? That poem was the preface to
an anthology Longfellow published in 1848, called *The Waif*.
The anthology drove Edgar Allan Poe mad with grief and
rage and spite. Why? Because it was a fancy, expensive Christmas present of a book, a book of the North, and Longfellow
hadn't included any of Poe's own poems. Poe had written
Longfellow fan letters—and then he was left out of *The Waif*.
Left out on purpose, Poe believed. And Poe was right. In his
review of the anthology, Poe said that Longfellow had deliberately omitted the American writers he owed so much to.
And then Poe went on a crusade, charging Longfellow with
theft, writing pseudonymous letters. Longfellow's rejection
had pushed him over the edge.

And yet it was all for the best, perhaps. Out of those feelings of miserable exclusion and persecution and lucklessness, Poe wrote "The Raven."

I got home and sat in the kitchen staring at an empty bowl. Paul Chowder's bowl of poetry.

WHAT I'M STARTING to realize is that I don't want a bowl of poetry. I want, more than anything, a bowl of cold potato salad with bits of parsley in there and the skins of the potato and the flesh of the potato but somewhat confused by the presence of the mayonnaise. I want to own a summer-sized drum of mayonnaise. Roz always used to buy a double-big jar of Hellmann's mayonnaise to celebrate summer. I want there to be cold potato salad in the empty bowl. Roz's potatoes held the cold of the fridge inside them, like chewable ice cubes. But there isn't any potato salad.

The mouse came out about ten-thirty p.m. I was still sitting at the kitchen table and I heard a tiny rattle and I saw him climb into the box made of squashed pulp that held the last stalk of blueberries. I'd picked one bunch of unripe blueberries on their stems in order to remember the different colors they have before they turn smoky blue. There are pale greens and pale pinks—Rubensesque colors that you don't expect blueberries to have because you think of blueberries as these smoky heavy bosomy black things in leaf shadow waiting to be plucked. But they're very light and green and springlike in their unripeness. And then they ripen and turn blue-black and finally go all wrinkly and raisinous. The mouse emerged from the stove and did his funny jerky rushing worried progress, branching here and there, retreating, advancing, and finally he made it across past the baking-soda box and the detergent bottle and up on the splash guard, and then he went down into the sink, and up from there into the drainer, and then he climbed into the pulp box and found the bunch of blueberries inside, and he dragged it back up into the stove.

When he came out again I tried to catch him with a plastic pitcher, but he climbed up the curtain and ran along the curtain rod and got away.

Here's the tune I made up for Poe's "Raven." It goes:

Raymond helped me disassemble the bed in Nan's guest room and move it out, and I went to Home Depot and strapped several hundred dollars' worth of pine planks to the roof rack. I bought a new saw blade, and flooring nails with long spirals graven into them so that they'd grip the subfloor better. I felt full of joyful purpose. A floor is a permanent thing. I was putting in a floor for my neighbor Nanette, and getting paid for it.

My finger bothered me a little bit when I was getting a nail started, till I learned to hold it a different way, the way somebody—maybe William Holden—smoked a cigarette. Raymond turned out to have a knack for carpentry. As did Nan, in fact. The three of us stapled down a layer of blue sheeting over the subfloor, and Nan cut around the edge with a retractable knife as if cutting off the excess of a piecrust. Then the planks started going in. We nailed all afternoon. We drank lemonade and talked about zombie movies, and zombie novels, and zombies in video games, and then we nailed some more. Raymond got his music player going, and we sang "Zombie Jamboree." I pointed out the off-rhyme in the song: "belly to belly" and "stone dead already." They were mildly interested. I also made a few mistakes of measurement that Nan saved me from. She had a good spatial sense, which carried us successfully through the tricky area around the bathroom door.

Chuck, Nan's boyfriend, appeared late in the afternoon, and I got him a hammer and a cupful of nails and he nailed, too, for a while. He was a perfectly decent guy. He is an engineer who works at the Navy Yard in Kittery caring for nuclear-powered submarines. He and his friends pull the nuclear engines out and change their spark plugs and bang their carburetors with wrenches and then slide the engines back in place. With Chuck there we talked about fractions of an inch and acceptable degrees of gap between boards, and we politely debated which length of board to use next.

When we were almost done I paused, sprawled on my elbow on the floor, thinking about the song of the nails. There were four hammers going now, each with a different speed of hammering. A nail starts by sounding low because there's more length of nail to vibrate, but as more and more of it disappears into the wood, its pitch gets higher and more strained. It goes *bong, bang, bing, bink*. And then, at the very end, just after the highest-pitched note, there are two or three confident wide low smacks when the nailhead has touched down and you're hitting the whole floorboard—*whang, whang, whang*. We all wanted to sound like good nailers, and we all did sound like good nailers—and I think we were content in the midst of that happy racket.

Just before I left, Chuck asked me why I was publishing an anthology of rhyming poems.

"It seemed like it would help somehow," I said.

Chuck said, "Are you making a statement? Are you saying that free verse is a bad thing?"

I said no, I didn't think I was, not really. My own poems were free verse, after all. But then again my own poems sickened me, so I was confused.

"Are you editing the anthology out of self-hatred?" Chuck pursued.

I smiled. "Yes, Chuck, I think that's it."

"What's the best poem ever written?" asked Nan.

I told her I couldn't answer that. "One poem I liked recently was James Fenton's 'The Vapour Trail.' "

" 'The Vapour Trail,' " said Chuck. "I'll check it out."

Nan walked me out to the deck and wrote out a check. What a nice sound it was to hear her tearing it out of her checkbook, while the frogs chirred away.

"I hear you singing in the barn sometimes," she said.

"Oh, sorry," I said.

"Roz told me she was at her wits' end because you were up in that barn for weeks singing away, not writing."

"Yes, but I'm doing better now. I'd like her to come back. If you talk to her, will you let her know that?"

"Sure," said Nan. "Thanks for the floor."

I WOKE UP after a nap. It was dark and very late. I found a pen and turned to the back of Mary Oliver's book of poems, and I wrote: "People I'm jealous of." I wrote:

—James Fenton
—Sinead O'Connor
—Lorenz Hart
—Jon Stewart
—Billy Collins.

"Billy" Collins, indeed. Charming chirping crack whore that he is. No, that's incorrect—I know nothing about him.

177

I know only my own jealousy. I'm not jealous of Merwin, though, and I'm not jealous of Mary Oliver. And I'm not jealous of Howard Moss. And I'm not jealous of Elizabeth Bishop. They're beyond all jealousy.

Yes, I wish I were a different person. Yes, I'm attacked by my embarrassments that are like those flying antibodies in *Fantastic Voyage* that glue themselves to the bad man's face when he swims out of the arterial spaceship. Yes, I sometimes have terrifying dreams in which a cat I've never seen before attacks a mouse and bites it and bites it, until I can hear its tiny neck make a popping sound. I pull the cat gently away and I take my shirt off and ball it up, and I prop the hurt mouse up against a balled-up shirt, and the mouse turns into a wan woman who talks to me in a laborious cheerful whisper in her brokenness. I want her to live. She says: "It's just impossible for me to live after what I've been through with that cat."

Oh, plot developments. Plot developments, how badly we need you and yet how much we flee from your clanking boxcars. I don't want to ride that train. I just want to sit and sing to myself. I want everything to be all right.

What if sometime Roz let me hold her breasts again? Wouldn't that be incredible? Those soft familiar palm-loads of vulnerability—and I get to hold them? That's simply insane. Inconceivable.

12

Sometimes I'll spend an hour writing a tiny email. I work on it until I've created the illusion that I've dashed it off in three minutes. If I make a typo, I let it stand. Sometimes in fact I correct the typo without thinking, and then I back up and re-type the typo so that it'll look more casual. I don't know why.

Swinburne didn't have that problem with email. Swinburne was remarkably prolific. In fact, he glutted the world with verse. He died in 1909, which is really the crucial year in the war between rhyme and unrhyme. Rhyme won each engagement before then. 1909 was the year, as we know, that Marinetti published his Futurist manifesto on the front page of *Le Figaro*. Futurism became all the thing in London, among the sophisticates. A little splinter group of tough-talking converts began meeting. They called themselves the Secession Club. Some of them wrote for a certain magazine, *The New Age,* whose editor was a man named Alfred Orage. Orage believed that rhyme and meter were the ruff collars and doublet jackets of poetry—mere fashions, superfluities. In the Secession Club there was a man named Flint and a man named Hulme and a man named Storer. And a man named Ezra Pound.

Swinburne was the greatest rhymer who ever lived, and Futurism was the breaking open and desecrating and graffiting of Swinburne's tomb.

How much do you know about Swinburne? Probably not that much. Tiny little guy. Nervous. Brilliant. Red hair. Loved babies, loved peering into perambulators. Wrote some exceptionally mawkish verse about babies. Deaf for the last twenty years of his life, and still writing poetry in the silence. Nobody had much to say about him when I was in college. He was like Vachel Lindsay, out of fashion. Browning? Sure. Meredith? Sure. Hardy? Sure. Dickinson? Sure. But Swinburne was not part of the big sweep.

And even now—take a look at this book. I'll block off the title so you have to guess what it is. Familiar design, I daresay. The little dude at the chalkboard? Yes, it's *Poetry for Dummies.* And it isn't a bad book. Do you know how hard it is to write a book like this? It's so hard. It's a terrible struggle; you fight with the Balrog through flame and waste and worry and incontinence and tedium. The Balrog of too-much-to-say. I've always liked the dummies books. I've got *Photoshop for Dummies,* and I learned a lot from it. The dummies' day may be passing, though. Too much yellow all over Barnes & Noble.

But now let's try something. Let's look up Algernon Charles Swinburne in the index of *Poetry for Dummies,* shall we? I've already done this so I know what's going to happen. But let's try it.

See that? Swinburne's not in the index. Algernon Charles Swinburne has been left out of *Poetry for Dummies.* And that's what I mean. Swinburne, the nineteenth century's King of Pain, the greatest rhymer in the history of human literature, has been lost to casual view. Without Swinburne, Lorenz Hart and Gershwin and Dorothy Field and the Great American Songbook would not sound the way they sound. And modernism would not have had the thrilling negative energy it had. You can't understand what all those early modern Futurist poets were in revolt against if you don't know about him. Swinburne says:

> If you were queen of pleasure
> And I were king of pain

Doesn't that give you a strange shudder? "If you were queen of pleasure (rest), and I were king of pain (rest),"

> We'd hunt down love together,
> Pluck out his flying-feather,

And teach his feet a measure,
And find his mouth a rein;
If you were queen of pleasure,
And I were king of pain.

Pretty good, eh? What is it? It's a four-beat line—three beats and a rest. Good with an inevitable step-slide of goodness to it.

Swinburne loved the old playwrights, where everyone ends up sprawled in a bloody heap. Once when he was drunk at the British Museum, he had some sort of seizure and cut his head and had to be carried out unconscious and bleeding by the guards. He had a decent shot at the poet laureateship, since he was far and away the most gifted living poet, but he didn't make it. Tennyson died and he, Swinburne, was quietly not chosen. Tennyson was morbid and strange, but Queen Victoria had been able to straighten his collar. And Tennyson had obliged by flipping on all the spigots and filling tankards with blank verse about King Arthur and the Round Table. But Swinburne couldn't be cleaned up. His collar couldn't be straightened. He was too strange, too sexually unaligned. One of his poems had to be printed with asterisks in place of half a stanza. All about "large loins."

What he could do was rhyme better than anybody. Deaf? Didn't matter. He heard what he needed to hear. Not only did he rhyme, he danced new dance steps while he rhymed. He mixed rhythms in a way nobody had done before. He was good at a certain kind of crooning, singing pulse, with the rhymes coming *poom, pom, ching, chong.* Nobody else came close to him in this. His sound was everywhere. It was trance music. It went around and around in your brain.

> A land that is lonelier than ruin,
> A sea that is stranger than death
> Far fields that a rose never blew in,
> Wan waste where the winds lack breath

Try writing your own couplets or rondeaus or what-you-wills after you've spent a day reading Swinburne. It's not easy. Louise Bogan was swimming in Swinburne's music when she began. Archibald MacLeish said in a letter that he'd gotten Swinburne in his head and couldn't get rid of him. Sara Teasdale said Swinburne had invented a new kind of melody. John Masefield said he was possessed by Swinburne and by Swinburne's teacher, Dante Gabriel Rossetti. Even Ezra Pound started off by writing Swinburne imitations—till he turned on him. A. E. Housman said that Swinburne's rhyming facility was unparalleled: "He seemed to have ransacked all the treasuries of the language and melted down the whole plunder into a new and gorgeous amalgam." You can hear Swinburne muttering behind the curtain in Dylan Thomas—"Altarwise by Owl Light" is a drunken version of Swinburne.

And Swinburne's big problem was that he wrote way, way, way too much. Any selection from his poetry is just a hint of the fluently tumbled profusion. Every song, every poem that he wrote was fully five times as long as it should have been. The rhymes and chimes kept coming. Internal, external. That's why he's so important to the twentieth century. Swinburne was like the application of too much fertilizer to a very green lawn.

THAT HAPPENED to one of my neighbors, Alan. Alan lives on the far side of Nan. His lawn glowed—it was a perfect malachite green. No weeds, uniform blade density, always mowed to the right height. He thought a lot about it. He tolerated my lawn, but I suspect that it made him unhappy. My lawn has weedy areas, pussy clover, dandelions. Roz told me that's what it's called, pussy clover. She knows the names of many plants. I let some of it grow tall because I like it. But Alan wanted his grass pure.

About five summers ago, Alan applied some kind of special very expensive fertilizer. He thought: This is going to take my lawn to the next level of lushness. But it must have been a bad bag, because a week after he applied it you could see big brownish yellow patches where something had gone wrong. The patches spread. They merged. Alan's lawn died. For two years after he applied it, the turf glinted like gold Brillo pads. There was no green left in it, and when you walked on its edge, it made a crunching sound of death. I don't think even the earthworms were alive underneath.

This isn't exactly what happened to poetry. Poetry didn't die. But Swinburne did drive his two-wheeled rhyme-spreader wagon all over the nineteenth century, and by the end of it he had gone back and forth and back and forth with his stanzas and his quatrains and his couplets and his lyrics and his parodies and everything else. It seemed like every word in English that could be rhymed in some melodious way he had rhymed. Some of the words, like "sea" and "rain," he'd rhymed hundreds of times. Rhyme words can't be used up, but even so, this was too much.

It took Alan years to get his grass back. Only this year is it again looking green and almost perfect. Poetry is still recovering from Swinburne.

I SAT AT THE KITCHEN TABLE with a tray that came from an order of Chinese food in front of me—clean—on which tiny beads rolled around. I tied a knot in the jeweler's wire. It's made of very fine wire threads woven together somehow so that it doesn't kink the way real wire does, but it's very strong.

I started to bead. The verb made sense. I was beading. What you do is pick up a bead and turn it for a while between the huge clumsy pillows of your good finger and your thumb, looking for the hole. You turn it until the shadow of the hole, or the light appearing through the hole, comes into view, and then you know where to insert the end of the wire. As soon as it's on, you lose interest in it and let it slip down and away, and you're on to the next one. Revising is difficult.

What I thought about was piecework. About the people who begin a set of beads, and then count, and are in the middle, and then they're done, and they pick up another string and start again. What kind of life would that be? Not bad as long as you weren't too rushed. I could string beads for a living. I kept thinking of the phrase "beads on a string."

The necklace got longer until finally I thought it might be long enough and I put it on and looked at myself in the mirror. I didn't look good, and it was still too short for Roz, who looks best with a medium length of beads. So I added another two quatrains, and then I started to get the feeling that I'd reached the end—a feeling I know from writing. I looped the thread through the magnet clasp, and then back through the crimping bead, and I took the pliers and crimped hard and cut off the extra thread. When they were done I put them in tissue paper and wrapped them, and I had a present ready for Roz. But I didn't know if I should give it to her.

I'M STILL PACKING UP my anthologies. Here's another one—Bullen's *Shorter Elizabethan Poems*. It's blue and heavy and dusty. Anthologies should be blue, I think. Although I love the anthology by Ted Hughes and Seamus Heaney, *The Rattle Bag*. It's green with the "ff" of the Faber logo all over it. The *Staying Alive* anthology is brown, and it has a girl's face on the cover. It's probably the best anthology that is mostly un-rhyme. In fact, *Staying Alive* may be the best poetry anthology ever.

I bought *Shorter Elizabethan Poems* for twelve dollars from a used-book store in Portsmouth. The first song—a.k.a. poem—in it is by William Byrd, the lute player, from 1588, and I think it's probably the song that Ted Roethke had turning around in his head when he wrote his villanelle, the one that starts "I wake to sleep and take my waking slow." William Byrd says: "I kiss not where I wish to kill, / I fain not love, where most I hate, / I break no sleep to win my will."

Do you notice those one-syllable words? The Elizabethans really understood short words. Each one-syllable word becomes a heavy, blunt chunk of butter that is melted and baked into the pound cake of the line. The first essay on how to write poems in English came out in 1587, by George Gascoigne. Gascoigne said that to write a delectable poem you must "thrust as few words of many syllables into your verse as may be." The more monosyllables, the better, he said. Roethke learned that lesson, as had Tennyson and Léonie Adams and lots of other people. One time Roethke danced around the room saying, "I'm the best god-damned poet in the USA!"

Here's another odd anthology I own: *The Poet's Tongue.* It's brown, not blue, and it's edited by W. H. Auden and John Garrett. It's interestingly arranged. The names of the poets don't appear with their poems. Everything's quoted anonymously. The only way you find out who wrote what is by looking up the numbers in the table of contents. At first this is slightly irritating, but then it becomes freeing. *The Poet's Tongue* was published in 1935 in England, and most of the bookstores in New York didn't have a copy for sale. But the Holiday Bookshop, on East Forty-ninth Street, did.

I know this because 1935 was the year that Louise Bogan and Ted Roethke had their long-shadowed love affair. Ted Roethke was younger than she was—very eager and ambitious. Louise Bogan was an established New York person, who'd worked at Brentano's bookstore. Who'd struggled. She didn't have a whole lot of money. She reviewed poems for *The New Yorker,* and I think she also helped them pick which poems to publish, too. She'd been married, she was no longer married, and she was prone to fits of depression, bouts of drinking, all the usual ills.

And Roethke impressed her as a poet of talent—"slight but unmistakable," she said. Moreover, they found that they really liked each other. So they had their lost weekend together, drinking quarts of liquor and doing every wild fucky thing that you can imagine that two manic-depressive poets might do. And she bloomed, as she said to her arguing-buddy Edmund Wilson, not like any old rosebush, but like a Persian rosebush.

Afterward she wrote an affectionate letter to Roethke. She was fonder of him than she wanted to allow herself to be. She knew he was too young for her, and she also knew, because she was a sensible and observant woman, that he was mentally ill, and selfish in that ambitious smart-boy way, and that he was even more of a ransacker of liquor lockers than she was, and that he was any number of things that would make him impossible to live with. But she still had fond feelings.

What she said was that she'd been paid $7.50 by *The New Yorker* for a poem that she'd written, called "Baroque Comment." Not seventy-five dollars—seven dollars and fifty cents. This is the middle of the Depression. And then she said—and this is why I love Louise Bogan—then she said exactly what she spent the money on.

She bought three things: a bar of soap, a new fountain pen, and a bottle of whiskey. And then she still had two dollars and fifty cents left over, after buying those three things— the pen to write poems with, the bottle of whiskey to drink in order to write the poems, and the soap in order to take on the world as a newly clean, thinking, feeling poet. She weighs whether she should buy some fancy food, but no: she remembers a certain recently published anthology that she's heard good things about. An anthology edited by Auden and Garrett, *The Poet's Tongue*. So she rushes over to the Holiday Bookshop. "And I bought the damn thing," she says. And she writes some of her best poems after this point. Including the first stanza of "Roman Fountain." This is probably the best, happiest moment of her poetic life, right here, while she's writing the letter to Ted Roethke, knowing she's got new poems waiting inside her.

In fact the letter may be better than any poem she wrote, though she wrote some good ones. But we wouldn't be interested in reading the letter unless she'd written the poems. So once again it's terribly confusing. You need the art in order to love the life.

I woke up at noon wondering why my face gets so flushed when I give readings. I wish it didn't. I hate my stupid grinning blushing pleading face.

A few people go to poetry readings because they like to hear poems read aloud in public. But most people go because they want to be poets themselves. In fact, most people who read poetry are reading it because they want to write it. They want to draw from you whatever you have, and once they've expeller-pressed your essence they want to move on to somebody else. They're ruthless that way. That goes on for a while and then eventually they come back around. The poets that would-be poets come back to after they've gotten through their phase of ripping and running—those are the poets that will last. The tortoises. Stanley Kunitz has a great poem about an old slow tortoise "reviewing its triumphs."

My dog was sleeping on the rug near the bed, and when he shifted I could hear his collar go clink. And I thought, So what if there are some broken veins in my cheek? So what if I look like some wind-worn fisherman, or golf caddy, from the Western Isles? So what if I stay up late eating sesame chicken and watching back-to-back episodes of *Dirty Jobs?* The rhubarb plant has grown an enormous seed stalk. It seems to want to say something to me. So what? I can't keep up with these nature lovers. It all just has to come elbowing out, and if a poem is a mistake it'll be clear that it's a mistake, and I won't collect it. There's something narcissistic in the phrase "collected poems." Who's collecting them? The poet. How hard is that? That's not a real collection. Now if he had made a collection of water fountains, or of oven mitts, that would be a collection. Or if he'd collected editions of *Festus,* the long mad poem written somewhere in the nineteenth century by a lost soul named Bailey—that would be an achivement. But collecting your own poems? What's so great about that? And mixing and mingling them in with some new? New *and* Collected Poems? Oh, well! Good job. Nice going.

I flip a lot through the biographical notes in the anthologies, and I find out who was alive when I was in my twenties, when I could have known them. I could have known Léonie Adams, I think. I could have known Louise Bogan, almost. I could have known Ted Roethke, a little earlier. Well, no—Roethke died when I was about ten I think. That's out. And if I had known him, what would it have mattered? Would I have become a better poet if I'd taken his class at the University of Washington and watched him climb out the window and stand on the outside ledge, working his way around the corner of the building, making crazy faces at his students through the glass? Maybe so.

The woman who was my French tutor in Paris was a great admirer of Mark Strand. She was a frayed, delicate, elegant woman, divorced. She would say her hero's name, in her gorgeous juicy accent, holding her fingers together: "Mark Strand—he is simply the top." And I would say, Okay, I'll have to check him out. Later I did check him out, and I thought he was fine but not great. But he was exceedingly good-looking, I could see that. A real Charlton Hestonian face, one of those hellishly handsome poets. James Merrill was another, and back then I lumped W. S. Merwin in with them. They were practically J. Crew models before there were J. Crew models. But that's not right, because Merwin has genius as well as looks. Merwin's late poetry gives me hope.

I feel everything breaking up inside me. I can't rhyme, and I don't believe in writing plums anymore. I don't even know the names of many common plants. What is a zinnia? I don't remember. What is pale jessamine? I don't know. Mary Oliver's got deer waking her up in the field in the early morning by licking her face. She's got grasshoppers eating sugar out of her hand. This just doesn't happen to me. I do know what a poppy looks like. It looks like a coffee filter but open and yellow-orange-red. Sometimes I think knowing the names of everything is overrated. It takes away the sense that each thing is itself and not part of some clique. But names help you see things, too, and remember them better.

I can remember her white living room, this tutor who almost taught me to talk in French, and her modern white fiberglass chair with a purple cushion. There was one lesson where we had a conversation, and she told me that I had made a distinct advance. But then I fell back. My shyness killed me in the end. I hated to speak wrong. Wrongly? I hated making simple mistakes. I hated not being able to speak quickly. One French guy at a bar wanted several of us to "faire le parachutisme." He said it was easy, you just jumped out of a plane. I said it sounded very exciting but no, thank you. He said, "I'm not a homo." I said it's not a question of whether or not you're a homo, I just don't want to jump out of a plane.

I called Roz and told her about the reading in Cambridge. She said she wished she could come, but she couldn't. I asked her how things were going. She said she was busy. I asked her if she missed me at all, at any time of the day or night. "Some, yes," she said. I thought that was a good sign.

WHEN SHOULD I give the beads to her? Maybe wait? Maybe give her the gift of not having to occupy her mind with my obvious wish to woo her back? Once when we were first going out she gave me a really big blue umbrella with about a hundred red cartoon monkeys on it. I left it on the train and then a man holding a cellphone ran after me and said, "I think you left this on the train." So I still have it.

What would Aphra Behn advise me to do? Aphra Behn understood love. She was the first woman in England to live by her writing. People set her love poems to music. She spied in Holland for the king, and then the king didn't pay her. She was always making love into a person: "Love in fantastic triumph sat," she wrote, "While bleeding hearts around him flowed."

Victorian women didn't like Aphra Behn. Back in the 1880s, there was a New Hampshire writer, Kate Sanborn, who published an interesting book on women's humor. She called it *The Wit of Women*. It cost me forty dollars to buy it from a dealer in Wellesley. "Aphra Behn," Sanborn said, "is remembered only to be despised for her vulgarity. She was an undoubted wit, and was never dull, but so wicked and coarse that she forfeited all right to fame." Why did they hate her so much—just because she wrote a quick poem about a seduction on a riverbank?

Let's pack it up. I've packed another two boxes. Here's a poetry packing tip for you. Make two load-bearing stacks or towers of books in two diagonally opposite corners of the box. The two stacks must go right up to the top edge of the box. That way it won't crumple and slump—you can pile boxes four or five high, and the weight of the top box will be transmitted down through the two stacks of the one below and the one below that.

13

I STARTED TO GET SLEEPY in the middle of the afternoon, so I went out and mowed half the lawn. That always wakes me up. And as I mowed, I thought, The interesting thing is that you can start mowing anywhere. The lawn will get done no matter where you start mowing. And that seemed like an important discovery.

Because so often I think when I'm writing a poem that I need to start in some specific spot. Where I begin becomes so important that I never begin. I've been trying to write a poem about a time when Roz wore a pair of white pants.

I walked upstairs behind her
Staring at her stitched seams
Normally she wore black pants
But it was the last day of the year
That she could wear the white ones
So she did

Haaaaahhhh! I'm going to oxygenate myself. Haaaaaaah-hhh!

You can start anywhere. That's the thing about start-ing. If you start, you're in motion. If you don't start, you're nowhere. If you stop, you're nowhere. I have reached a cri-sis where I don't know where to start. It's arbitrary. I could start with sunlight on clapboards, because is there anything more beautiful than sunlight on clapboards? A strange word: "clapboards." It's one of those interestingly wrong words—it sounds flabby, like clabbered milk, when it's talking about something cleanly edged.

I wish I were happy in a disciplined way. Happy in a nondespairing way. I wish that I could spill forth the wis-dom of twenty years of reading and writing poetry. But I'm not sure I can. I've published poems, yes. That much is beyond question. And for a while I was pleased with the poems that I published. I felt that I understood why people write poetry. I understood the whole communal activity of writing and reviewing and extracting quotes to go on the paperback. "Moss has arrived, with next to no luggage, at mastery." Being part of the interfaith blurb universe.

And now it's like I'm on some infinitely tall ladder. You know the way old aluminum ladders have that texture, that kind of not-too-appealing roughness of texture, and that kind of cold gray color? I'm clinging to this telescoping ladder that leads up into the blinding blue. The world is somewhere very far below. I don't know how I got here. It's a mystery. When I look up I see people climbing, rung by rung. I see Jorie Graham, I see Billy Collins, I see Ted Kooser. They're all clinging to the ladder, too. And above them, I see Auden, Kunitz. Whoa, way up there. Samuel Daniel. Sara Teasdale. Herrick. Tiny figures, clambering, clinging. The wind comes over, *whssssew*, and it's cold, and the ladder vibrates, and I feel very exposed and high up. Off to one side there's Helen Vendler, in her trusty dirigible, filming our ascent. And I look down, and there are many people behind me. They're hurrying up to where I am. They're twenty-three-year-old energetic climbing creatures in their anoraks and goggles, and I'm trying to keep climbing. But my hands are cold and going numb. My arms are tired to tremblement. It's freezing, and it's lonely, and there's nobody to talk to. And what if I just let go? What if I just loosened my grip, and fell to one side, and just—*fffshhhooooow*. Let go.

Would that be such a bad thing?

I RAN OVER A ROCK with the lawnmower, now my lawnmower is broken. It doesn't start and I've bent the propeller shaft, which is something I can't fix, so that's two hundred dollars to the repair place, where they also sell baby chickens. And bags of chickenfeed. All this money is being swept from me. A faint breath of money somehow appears, a mist of money. I breathe it out into the air, and immediately it's sucked away by those who have entered into elaborate agreements with me that I haven't read.

I can do five chin-ups now, and I'm going to be helping my friend Tim out with painting his house. He's putting in a new door in back and painting the whole house a deep blue-black, and I'm going to make maybe fifteen hundred dollars helping him scrape and paint. Which means I'll be fine for next month, financially. He says that Haffner College won't have me back to teach writing. They are so right not to have me back.

Elizabeth Bishop wrote: "I am so sick of Poetry as Big Business I don't know what to do." None of the good poets believed in teaching. Auden said it was dangerous. Philip Larkin said that when you start paying people to write poems and paying people to read them you remove the "element of compulsive contact." Too bad Larkin's poems are so killingly down-bringing. I can't bear Larkin, not because he isn't a very good poet—he is a very good poet—but because anytime I get anywhere near him it's poison, I don't want to go on living. His acid is just too corrosive. I can't read his poems, but I can remember reading them with amazed undelight whenever I read his prose. So his poetry is still working on me indirectly.

Late in the afternoon I was talking to Tim on the phone about Queen Victoria when I heard a huge buzzing in the window. I said, "Tim, excuse me, I've got to go investigate this huge buzzing insect." I hung up and looked at it.

It was a waspy sort of creature with a long tubular abdomen that carried a herringbone pattern in yellow. Something that resembled a hypodermic syringe poked out its back end. I called Roz right away. I said, "I'm sorry to bother you, but remember that insect that you told me about once with the long herringbone abdomen?"

"Yes," she said.

I said, "It's on the windowsill in the dining room. It's got a huge long pointy thing hanging off its end and the point has snagged a strand of dust and it is so big that at first glance I thought it was two wasps mating."

"I know that one," she said.

"Do you know what it's called? I was thinking of writing something about it."

"Let me check," Roz said. She got her copy of the Audubon guide to New England bugs and birds and miscellaneous other things—the one with the frightening picture of the star-nosed mole—a book that used to lie on a little rusty table on our porch and now she has it, because it's her book. She had the happy sound in her voice that I remember from when she looks things up, a sound of optimism and soon-to-be-satisfied curiosity.

"Yes, here it is," she said after a minute. "It's called a

'pigeon horntail.' Here's what it says. 'Female has long ovi-positor.' "

"That's for sure," I said.

"It says the ovipositor 'deposits eggs deep into wood that larvae eat.' So you should probably take it out of the house because it wants to lay eggs that will eat the window-sill."

I thanked her and got a glass and a mailing envelope and scooted the soi-disant pigeon horntail into captivity. It buzzed, but it was tired from its struggle with the window dust. I walked with it down to the old lilac tree and let it go there. It could probably insert its ovipositor into one of the dead lilac branches. Roz once showed me something about old lilac wood: it has a streak of purple deep inside, as if it soaks some of the purpleness of the blossoms back into itself when they go.

I'M BACK from the reading in Cambridge. I "gave" the read-ing. Beforehand I took Smacko for a long walk, all the way to the salt pile and back, nodding and smiling at passersby, practicing being a public person. I washed out his water bowl very carefully so that all the invisible slime was gone, and I filled it with cold water while he panted, and I listened to him drink it. His collar clanked coolly against the brim. Then I drove to Cambridge.

As I drove I tried to do everything very gracefully. At the

tollbooth I fished my wallet out of my pocket and turned it over and opened it very gracefully, and I used just my thumb to lift a twenty out of its pouchy slumber. And when the toll-taker gave me back my change, I slid it into the change nook with practiced smoothness. I tore open a bag of vinegar-flavored potato chips and fished out one of them and turned it and touched my tongue to it, and drew it in without a sound. I sipped some coffee, and I looked to my left with an easy swivel, to see what kind of car was passing me. It was a blue Dodge Magnum—I forgave it with the gentlest of nods for being a big, arrogant car. Then I folded up the receipt for the coffee and potato chips and put it in my pocket with an extreme fluidity of gesture. And when I pushed the turn signal, I didn't click it all the way, but just held it with two fingers so that the circuit completed and it went click click, and then I released it. I turned on the CD player and listened to Carl Sandburg read aloud two lines of one of his poems and then I turned it off, with the subtlest pressure on the off button. I had the touch. I was good at what I did. And what I did was drive to poetry readings.

I found a place to park, and I was on time, and the book-store manager waited until there was a good crowd—twelve people, I think, maybe thirteen, including several bookstore employees, who were kind people who didn't dwell on the fact that their bookstore was going broke. I read some poems into the brightly lit corner of the store, including a new version of the one about Roz's white pants, and they didn't

sound too bad as I read them. The cash register began print-
ing its noisy nightly transaction summary just as I was finish-
ing "How I Keep from Laughing," which kind of wrecked it,
but that's all right.

A woman asked a question: did I agree or disagree with
Philip Larkin when he wrote that it was better to read poems
silently to yourself than hear them read aloud? I said, Well,
Larkin was right that when you heard a poem read aloud
you never knew how far you were away from the last line,
and you didn't know what the shape of the stanzas were,
but on the other hand if they didn't sound good when read
aloud then forget it. I said I found Carl Sandburg unread-
able on the page, but when I drove around listening to him
read in his wildly mannered way—"in the coooool, of the
toooooooombs, of Chicaaaahgo"—then I loved it. Sandburg
gives every syllable a special extra squeeze. I told them that
Sandburg was so incredibly popular at one point that he
had a secretary to help him answer his fan mail, and he'd go
through it and write "Send A" or "Send B" or "Send C" on
it, meaning that the secretary should type boilerplate letter
A or B or C as a reply. So there was something to reading
poems aloud.

I sold one book—a copy of *Worn*. A man came up and
said he'd bought all three of my books but he didn't have
them anymore because when he got married he decided to
clean out his shelves and he took a few hundred books to a
book dealer and the dealer gave him a ridiculously low price

but he took it. And now he was divorced and buying books again, and would I sign this one and this time he would keep it. So I did.

ON THE WAY back up Route 95 I sang along with Slaid Cleaves doing his song "Sinner's Prayer" until I couldn't stand it anymore and I called up Roz and left a message.

I said "Hello, I'm calling to give you a progress update. I've done the reading in Cambridge, check, and I'm almost done cleaning out my office, almost check, and my finger's healing up well—thank you for taking care of me that day— and the introduction is now progressing. So things are moving along. And I'm hoping you'll come back sometime and hang your tablecloths back on the line." And then I added: "And I just wonder if there's anyone who knows you like I do!" And then I couldn't talk any more, so I hung up.

One time when Roz was still with me I came home late from a reading in Madison, Wisconsin, and she was already asleep, and so was the dog. I kicked Smacko in the head by mistake in the dark, not too hard, but he made a little growly yelp, and I said I was sorry to him, and that woke Roz. I got in bed, and she smelled so smilingly sleepy that soon I had my hand on her hip and I said, "Baby, that is one big sexy hip."

She stirred and said, "Yikes, what's going on here?"

I said, "I don't know, what's going on with you?"

She turned and unbuttoned her pajama top over me, and I could see one of her breasts outlined in the orange light coming from the street. Her breasts didn't have to rhyme, but in fact they did rhyme.

THE MOUSE HAS COME OUT from the control panel of the stove, and he's making a lot of noise by scraping things off of the burners with his mouse teeth. He wasn't discouraged by the Boraxo I sprinkled around, or the spritzes of Windex. I set up a humane trap of a toilet-paper tube with a dab of peanut butter on the end, balanced tippily on the counter out over the trash can, but he wasn't fooled. He's scooting silently across the counter now, in search of the Lava soap, which he gnaws at. He eats the corners first. Imagine eating lava soap. His head is very long, like a weasel's head. He lives in fear. If I lift my arm he dashes back. But then he creeps out again. He's bolder than he used to be. He doesn't know whether it's okay to be a part of my life or not. And I would be quite happy for him to be out and about, and even gnawing at my soap, if he wasn't constantly taking little craps everywhere. What a foolish thing for him to do. I may have to buy a trap from a guy in Sandwich, Massachusetts. It runs on a maze principle and is supposedly not traumatic for the mouse. It's called the Mouse Depot. I can't have fifteen mouse droppings on the stove every single night, and that's sad because I'll miss him.

You know what? I could write forever. This is me. This is me you're getting. Nobody else but me.

You may not want me. I don't care. I want you to have me. That's the way it works. I'm here giving and you're there taking. If you are there. I can't know and you are probably falling asleep. You have many reasons for reading what you read. You want to, quote, "keep up." Good luck. You want to know what somebody who was rumored to be on the short list for poet laureate of the United States would write after it turned out that he wasn't in fact chosen. What does he write about then? Hass was chosen, and Pinsky was chosen, and Kooser was chosen, and Simic was chosen. And Kay Ryan was chosen. Goody.

Goody for all of them. It's all about a piece of steak. There's that Jack London story, about the old tired boxer who almost wins a comeback, but he doesn't because he didn't have enough money to buy that one piece of steak he hungered for the day before—the steak that would have given him the strength to land the big punch. So he's beaten. He's smacked around. He bleeds. He fails. That's me. If I could only have written a good flying spoon poem back three years ago when I first wanted to, I might be poet laureate right now. Maybe. Probably not. But maybe. I might be going to fancy diplomatic receptions and talking to flirty women from the Spanish embassy with no shoulder straps and eating steamy vulval canapés that leap into my mouth practically of their own volition. I would be part of the Washington evening scene, and

I'd be sent invitations to receptions engraved on heavy stationery, with very sharp corners and skimpy tissue overlays that would fall and glide low and long across the floor. I'd own a black-tie outfit. But it has all happened a different way. I'm up here in Portsmouth, city of brick sidewalks. And I like this city a lot. But I'd love those canapés, too.

14

I'VE JUST HAD A SHARP FLARE of an emergency, but I think it's now under control. What happened was I remembered that I should put my passport in my briefcase so I wouldn't forget it when I went to the airport to go to Switzerland.

And then suddenly I wondered: Is my passport possibly out of date? I thought, no, it can't possibly have expired. I looked in my top drawer among the socks and the underpants and my fragile folded birth certificate, and there it was. I flipped it open with my paperback-holding fingers and looked inside and there was my more-than-ten-years-younger face, and yes: it was expired. My flight is on Monday night, and this was Thursday.

I called the federal government of the United States, and a nice woman who worked there made an appointment for me in Boston on Monday morning at nine-thirty.

You SEE, this is what I'm up against. This little book here. Published by Farrar, Straus, which publishes Elizabeth Bishop. It's James Fenton, *An Introduction to English Poetry*. Very nice indeed. In it he says some true and interesting things and some false things.

We can't blame him for saying the false things, because he's saying what everybody has always said from the abysm of time. First he says that iambic pentameter is preeminent in English poetry. No it is not. No it is not. Iambic pentameter is an import that Geoffrey Chaucer brought in from French verse, and it was unstable from the very beginning because French is a different stress universe than Middle English and it naturally falls into triplets and not doublets. No, the march, the work song, the love lyric, the ballad, the sea chantey, the nursery rhyme, the limerick—those are the preeminent forms, and all those have four beats to them. "Away, haul away, boys, haul away together, / Away, haul away boys, haul away O." Fenton's own best poems use four-beat lines.

And then Fenton says that iambic pentameter is, quote, "a line of five feet, each of which is a ti-tum. As opposed to a tum-ti."

And that's what they all say. Fenton doesn't know what he knows. He's written beautiful iambic pentameter lines. His ear knows that there's more to it than that. And he is just one of an endless line of people who say that an iambic pentameter line is made up of five feet, or five beats. And it isn't. An iambic pentameter line is made up of six feet. Or rather five feet and one empty shoe—i.e., a rest. Unless the line is forcibly enjambed and then, to my ear, it sounds bad. Keats, bless his self-taught genius soul, came up with some scary enjambments. "My heart aches, and a drowsy numbness pains," next line, "My sense."

BUT LET'S GET the Sharpie out. And let's take a look at a real iambic pentameter line. Two of them, in fact, from Dryden. I'm going to write them out for you. This is the couplet that I copied out in my notebook, as I think I mentioned. It's called a heroic couplet—and Dryden was the one who really made it work in English. He forced its preeminence. He used it to write what he called "heroic plays," and he used it to translate Virgil's *Aeneid,* which is about the heroic deeds of gods and men. And after him came Pope and everyone else. The couplet goes like this. I'll sing it.

All hu man things are sub ject to de cay / And
when fate sum mons mon archs must o bey.

Now, the way we're taught to talk about these two lines is to say that they are in iambic pentameter. There are two parts to this. First, "iambic." And second, "pentameter."

"Iambic" is a Greek word that in English just means an upbeat. The iambic conductor puffs out his man chest, lifts his batoned hand up, and everybody sees the eighth note hovering there before the bar line on their music stands, and the string tremolo builds, and the mallets of the tympani blur, and the chord swells, and crests, and gets foamy at the ridge, and then the baton comes down and a big green glittering word-wave crashes down on the downbeat. Ya-*ploosh*. Ka-*posh*. "All human things." That's the iamb. It's a kind of sneeze. Iambs can begin four-beat lines or so-called pentameter lines, which are really six-beat lines. "Oh *who* can from this dungeon raise." "A *soul* enslaved so many ways." "And *what* is Art whereto we press." "The *world* is too much with us." "I *met* a man who wasn't there." Let's see, what are some more? "The *wed*ding guest, he beat his breast." "My *little* horse must think it queer."

Dang, I keep wanting to use shorter lines as my examples. Which is my point.

But let's see, let's see. "I *should* have been a pair of ragged claws." Prufrock. Iambic pentameter. "When *I* have fears that I may cease to be." Keats, iambic pentameter. "Mere *an*archy is loosed upon the world." Yeats, iambic pentameter. "And *slen*der hairs cast shadows, though but small." Dyer. "If *you* can keep your head when all about you." Kipling. "The *art* of losing isn't hard to master." Elizabeth Bishop. "They *flee* from me who sometime did me seek." Et cetera, et cetera. "Et cetera" is an iambic rhythm, if you pronounce it the way the French do. And iambs are extremely common. The first syllable is an upbeat to the line, and the rhythm is a game of tennis—it's that basic duple rhythm, badoom, badoom, badoom.

Now one problem with "iamb" as a name for this clearly audible upbeat phenomenon is that the word "iamb" isn't iambic, it's trochaic. A trochee is a flipped iamb. It's like a staple-crunch: *crunk*-unk. "Iamb" is trochaic. Isn't that the most ridiculous thing you ever heard? And we've tolerated and taught this impossible Greek terminology for centuries. If iamb were pronounced "I *am*!"—as a counterfactual—it would itself be iambic. "I *am* interested in what you're saying!" "I *am* going to take out the garbage!" "I think therefore I *am*!" You hear that? Then "iamb" would be a decent name for what's going on. Not a great name, but a decent name. But no, it isn't pronounced with the stress on the second syllable. And yet this is what we've got to work with. "Iambic" is the name for this sort of upbeat when it's found in a duple rhythm. Not in a triple rhythm. In a triple rhythm, there's another Greek word you can use, if you're inclined: "anapest." But in a double rhythm, a line that begins with an upbeat is iambic. If you follow me. Just saying all this creates a fog of brain damage.

But so much for the first part of the phrase, "iambic." Just set it and forget it. Don't worry about it. You can change an initial trochee to an iamb by adding an "And" or an "O." And you can flip around an iamb so that the line begins with a little triplet, or an eighth note and a sixteenth note, which happens a lot—as in "Season of mists and mellow fruitfulness." Or "Give me my scallop-shell of quiet." So the whole notion is fluid, and we don't need to dwell on it any longer. Some lines begin with an upbeat and some don't—that's all you need to know about the iamb.

BUT NOW FOR THE REAL THORNINESS: PENTAMETER. "All human things are subject to decay." That's the line. Then: "And when fate summons monarchs must obey." And you think, Okay, good, I see five stresses there, like five blackbirds on a power line.

①   ②   ③   ④   ⑤

All human things are subject to decay

Five little blackbirds. Ah, but there's a raven of a rest there at the end that you're not counting, my friend. If you say the two lines together, you'll hear the black raven. Listen for him:

①　　　②　　　③　　④　　⑤　　❻
All **hu**man **things** are **sub**ject **to** de**cay**　**CRAW!**

①　　　②　　　③　　④　　⑤　　❻
And **when** fate **sum**mons **mon**archs **must** o**bey**　**CRAW!**

If you leave out those raven squawks—those rests—and you only count the blackbirds on the line, you are not going to be able to say this couplet the way Mr. Dryden meant it to be said. Try it as a run-on. "All-human-things-are-subject-to-decay-and-when-fate-summons—" What? Who? Where am I? You see? It's just not right that way. You cannot have five stresses in a line and then jog straight on to the next line. If you do that, it sounds out of whack. It sounds horrible. It sounds like—enjambment.

Let's take another example of a heroic couplet. This one is from Samuel Johnson. He wrote it for his impoverished drunken friend Oliver Goldsmith.

①　　②　　③　　　④　　　⑤　　❻
How **small**, of **all** that **hu**man **hearts** en**dure**, (rest)

①　　　②　　③　　　④　　⑤　　❻
That **part** which **wars** or **kings** can **cause** or **cure**. (rest)

You've got to have the rests! There's no question about it. If you don't have the rests, you don't have a proper couplet. These are six-beat lines. So-called iambic pentameter is in its deepest essence a six-beat line.

Actually no, I take that back. It's not. In its very deepest, darkest essence it's a three-beat line. Here's where we get to the nub of it. Because people really only hear threes and fours, not sixes. Let's take a look at how this works. And to do it, we're going to up the pace a little bit. We're going to say some of these lines flowingly and fast, listening for the way they truly fall. And as we do, we're going to tap our feet in rhythm. Let's try it. Get your foot tapping with me, in a nice slow walking pace.

With me now: One——two——three. One——two——three. "How **small** of all that **hu**man hearts en**dure** (rest), the **part** which wars or **kings** can cause or **cure** (rest), all **hu**man things are **sub**ject to de**cay** (rest), and **when** fate summons **mon**archs must o**bey** (rest), that **time** of year thou **mayst** in me be**hold** (rest), When **yell**ow leaves or **none** or few do **hang** (rest), When **I** have fears that **I** may cease to **be** (rest), be**fore** my pen has **gleaned** my teeming **brain** (rest)." Are you with me? I feel like I'm making an exercise video.

What's happening is that if you tap your foot only to the big beats, you end up with a line of inner quadruplets chugging away in sync with three large stresses. You can chart it like this:

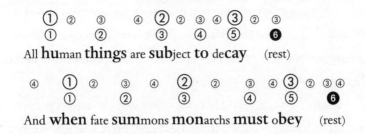

Looks like an air-balloon festival, does it not? But I hope it shows that what we call iambic pentameter is really, if you count the rest the way you must count it, a kind of slow waltz rhythm. You can leap around the room reciting so-called iambic pentameter to yourself and your leaps will fall in threes. You cannot make your leaps fall into fives. You need to add the rest. I'm telling you that this is true. No amount of reading and underlining any textbook about meter and seeing them go on and on about five beats is going to make that necessary sixth rest beat go away. It's there, and it's been there for centuries. And when poets forget that it's there, it hurts their poems.

15

MISTY AGAIN TODAY. A freakish mist lies over the land. My clothes are out on the clothesline, and they have been there for two days and they've started to get that wet-too-long smell.

Now, if I were a nineteenth-century poet, I would say that the freakish mist lay "o'er" the land. And that's one of those words, "o'er," that makes a modern reader feel ill. So what I do, to make the old poems feel true again—the good old poems—is very simple. This is another little tip for you, so get ready. I just pronounce "o'er" as "over," but I do it very fast, so you're gliding o'er the V, not really adding another syllable. Because that's really what it was, I think: it was a crude, printed representation of a subtle spoken elision that might well have had some of the vocal ghost of the V left in it.

There are rare times when it's absolutely necessary to say "o'er" without any V—as when, say, Macaulay rhymes it with "yore." But a lot of the time you can fudge it.

This trick will also work for "'tis" and "ne'er"—the other painful bits of poetic diction. When I'm reading a poem to myself, I just mentally change all the instances of "'tis" to "it's." And I give "ne'er" the "o'er" treatment—I just barely graze my teeth with my lower lip, while thinking V. It's like waving the vermouth bottle over the glass of gin. Try it, it may work for you.

After all, we don't want some mere convention of spelling to block our connection with the oldies. We want to hear them now as if they're being said now. And that tailcoated diction can really get in the way. It's bad. Not to mention the exclamation points everywhere. Lo! Great God! Just ignore them. If you say the poem aloud, they disappear.

The mouse climbed up the curtain again, and this time I got him to drop into the plastic pitcher. I took him out to the lilac bush and let him go in the mist.

I CALLED UP ROZ to ask her if there was anything she wanted from Switzerland. She told me she had the flu and wasn't thinking straight because she had a fever. I asked her if I

could bring over some chicken soup and crackers and gin-
ger ale, because I knew that's what she'd want. And she said,
"That would be nice. Also some chewable Motrin, the junior
kind, and a trashy magazine." So I went over to her apartment, which she'd painted five careful colors—and I helped
her sit up. She really had been quite sick, very feverish, hot,
confused. "I'm here to take care of you," I said, and I gave
her the chewable Motrin and a spoonful of soup, and she ate
a corner of a cracker.

"Let me think of cold things to cool you down," I said.
"Do you remember how you used to make that marvelously cold potato salad and we'd have it outside on the metal
table?"

She nodded. "On cool tin plates," she said. "That was
fun." Then she said she was going to sleep, and she thanked
me for coming by.

I MOWED more of the lawn. But first I cut away the thorny
brambles so that they wouldn't attack me as I mowed near
them. What I found was that grapevines were kinking their
spirals around the long, reaching, hooky bramble suckers.
The two plants had a little gentlemen's agreement going, like
the railroad companies and the real-estate speculators in the
old days, whereby they progressed together up the hill and
into the yard. I pulled some of their tanglement out of an
old, beleaguered lilac bush, and I got pricked a lot but I felt

I'd accomplished something. Then I mowed for an hour and chanted a stanza of Kipling as I mowed, from his poem about the undersea cables.

> The wrecks dissolve about us; (rest)
>> Their rust drops down from afar— (rest)
> Down to the dark, to the utter dark,
>> Where the blind white sea-snakes are. (rest)

When I was done mowing I drank a glass of iced coffee with some baking soda mixed into it to soften the burn. And I went up to my now half-empty bookcases in the hall and found Theodore Roethke's prose collection, *On the Poet and His Craft*. It's a small white book. On the cover is a picture of Roethke looking sad, as he always looked, sitting against a wall with a mysterious white graffiti hand-painted on it. The dustjacket is very soft on the top and the bottom edges because it has slid out of place and crunched into things. Holding this book always affects me strangely. It was put together by one of Roethke's colleagues, and it came out only a year or two after Roethke died. It's like standing in some little cemetery somewhere, staring at a small white gravestone in the grass.

In it was Roethke's review of his old flame, Louise Bogan. He adopts a formal tone—he keeps calling her Miss Bogan. And he quotes nice things from her poems—for instance he quotes "Roman Fountain." And he says, rightly, that the first stanza is good and the rest he doesn't care for as much. Bogan herself thought that. She said the poem was minor except for the first stanza. He includes some criticisms to show that he's a dispassionate reader and that he's not going to let their long-ago lost weekend influence what he says.

And then he says the Big Thing. He says that Louise Bogan's poetry will last "as long as the language survives." There it is. This was in one of the last reviews he wrote. It was what he hoped would be true of his own poetry.

Her poems will last as long as the language—ah, yes. That used to be, in the nineteenth century, a much-employed piece of literary praise. Macaulay used it several times. He said, for example, that Byron's poetry "can only perish with the English language." Mark Twain said that *Uncle Tom's Cabin* would "live as long as the English tongue shall live." Many lesser nineteenth-century reviewers used it. And it's a fearful phrase—it's an Ozymandian phrase. Because you have to ask: How long, in fact, will the English language last? Not that long maybe. Another three hundred years?

One day the English language is going to perish. The easy spokenness of it will perish and go black and crumbly— maybe—and it will become a language like Latin that learned people learn. And scholars will write studies of *Larry Sanders* and *Friends* and *Will & Grace* and *Ellen* and *Designing Women* and *Mary Tyler Moore,* and everyone will see that the sitcom is the great American art form. American poetry will perish with the language; the sitcoms, on the other hand, are new to human evolution and therefore will be less perishable. Some scholar will write, a thousand years from now: Surprisingly very little is known of Monica Mcgowan Johnson and Marilyn Suzanne Miller, who wrote the "hair bump" episode of *Mary Tyler Moore*. Or: Surprisingly little can be gleaned from the available record about Maya Forbes and Peter Tolan, who had so much to do with the greatness of *Larry Sanders*.

And even so, I want to lie in bed and just read poems sometimes and not watch TV. Regardless of what will or won't perish.

I SAT IN THE DRIVEWAY and read my old poems for about an hour in the morning. As I read them I had some driveway sand between my toes, and I felt the faceted grains rolling. And I had a combinatorial feeling. I was embarrassed but also impressed. I'd written a lot of poems, frankly. When you turn the page there is another poem. And there's another. And another. And they keep going. Somehow I have accumulated a whole bunch of poems. Each one had its itinerary—each had gone to a particular editor and gotten published somewhere, except for some that I kept back that I didn't want any editor to have, and some that no editor wanted, and then I'd collected them in a book.

I put the book down on the metal table, and I went inside and I tried to write about how a tablecloth catches the ottoman of the air as it settles down on a metal table. And now I'm back outside again sitting in the white plastic chair looking at the dew on the gas cap of my car. A fly wants to bite me on the ankle. The mosquitoes are all asleep. They're just not out at this hour. Only one biting fly. And a mourning dove, who blows through his thumbs to make that sound.

MY ANTHOLOGY has to have the right thickness. I do know that. It has to have that I'm-not-really-a-textbook textbook-ishness. It has to have a lot of love poems in it because in the end love poems are the best kind of poems. If it had a whole lot of love poems and was the right thickness, it might be adopted in college classes. September comes, and sleepy undergraduates all over the country are walking their diagonal paths to writing classes with *Only Rhyme* zipped away in their backpacks. I would have power and influence—maybe even a trickle of money. That's a motivator. Power and influence, baby. And maybe some of the poems I chose would make people happy. That would be my contribution. I want to include a Charles Causley poem, and a Wendy Cope poem, and a James Fenton poem. I haven't heard back from Fenton's publisher yet so I don't know if I'll get permission. I hope so.

The Fenton poem is "The Vapour Trail." I was going through a pile of old *New York Review of Books*'s last year and I saw the title and immediately my heart leapt up, because I always want to read a poem about a vapor trail. So I approached it with that kind of high hope. That feeling of maybe this will be the definitive vapor-trail poem. And it was. It was good, and it was sad, and it was exactly, precisely what you wanted a poem about a vapor trail to be. Exactly, precisely what you wanted a poem about anything to be, in fact. It was moving, and it sang, and it had love in it, and it got you. It grabbed at your love-and-fame vitals. I tore out the whole page from the *New York Review,* and I clamped it to the refrigerator with a magnet.

And yesterday I took it off the refrigerator and I made two copies of it. One I mailed to Nan with a Post-it saying, "This is the poem I mentioned." And one I mailed to Roz, saying, "This is a good one. Miss you, hope you're feeling better —P."

And as I mailed the Fenton poems out I thought: See that? It's happening. The transformation, the rediscovery, the renewal. It's happening already. It's so exciting. It's all cycling around. Fenton's been doing it. My little attempts to write poems that rhyme—unnecessary. My whole career—unnecessary. Because this Fenton poem is out. Good for him. Good for good old Jamesie. I thought of writing him a letter, and I thought, Well, you know, then he'll have to write me a letter, and it'll be one of those replies where he'll be compelled to say, "Coming from you, that's high praise indeed." Or not—and if he doesn't say "coming from you" I'll be hurt-feelinged, so I thought, Forget it. But I also thought: My life has been in vain and yet not in vain because I've had the pleasure of seeing the whole movement come full circle. I've lived through the thirty-year ascendancy of chaos and tunelessness, and things are moving back now. It was a mistake to suppress rhyme so completely, a mistake to forget about the necessary tapping of the toe, but it was a useful mistake, a beautiful mistake, because it taught us new things. It loosened people up and made other discoveries possible.

I don't have to say any of that in the introduction, though. The introduction can be quite short. Forty pages? Forget forty pages. How many people read introductions to poetry anthologies, anyway? Hardly anyone. I do, but I'm not normal. It doesn't actually matter what I say. Short is best. It should just read: "Welcome to this anthology of rhymed poetry by dead and living poets. I hope you find some things here you like. Thanks so much for your attention. And now—on with the show."

Only Rhyme would of course define me as an anthologist—i.e., as a lost soul who turned in despair to the publishing of other people's work—like old Oscar Williams. Old Father Oscar. Sure, Williams got a friendly blurb from Dylan Thomas, but everybody knew his warbling days were done. Still, I think I could live with that.

The real problem is that I've had to leave known poets out. Some of them are alive and old. A few of them I've met and like. They have strophed and sonneted and upheld the traditional ideals. All that's missing from their work is greatness—the elusive *rupasnil*. They're clumsy rhymers. They're over-enjambers. Their lines are clotted with wrongness of several kinds. They're following the old rules on paper, but they don't hear them—they don't understand the body-logic behind them. Some of them, when they discover that I've left them out, will be wounded. And I don't want to wound them.

If I don't write the introduction, then the anthology can't come out, and then the inept but well-meaning recent rhymers won't have their feelings hurt. Which would be better all around.

Tim called and said that he'd sent *Killer Queen* off to the publisher.

I WENT OVER to Roz's apartment with Smacko, because she was going to be taking care of him while I was in Switzerland. She was getting out of her car in the shade of a maple tree. She'd just come back from Red Leaf, a vegetable store out near Exeter. She lowered her head to the grocery bag she held and she breathed in. She said, "Don't you love the smell of brown paper bags filled with raw vegetables?"

I leaned and smelled inside the bag. "Yes, I like it very much," I said. Trying to stay on an even keel but feeling a lot of love for her and wanting to lie down on the sidewalk as a result.

She stood, smiling, waiting for me to say something more. I handed her the beads, wrapped droopily in tissue. "Just something I strung for you, don't open it now."

She thanked me, and then she tilted her face up and I kissed her quickly, pretend-perfunctorily. "Good luck in Switzerland," she said.

16

THE ADDRESS of the Tip O'Neill building is 10 Cause-way Street. It may be torn down soon, because it is one of the most wonderfully unsightly buildings ever con-structed. In the eighties they blew up a grand hotel that had gone seedy, and in its place they built this shrine to Congress-man Tip O'Neill. It houses all the federal offices—the office of Social Security, and the Firearms Legitimization Bureau, the Bioshock Informant Management Corps, and the Soy Protein Tax Credit Administration, and the Federal Security Corn Slab Ektachrome Mediocrity Desk, plus another twelve important outposts of American impotence. And it has wire-less Internet.

There was a guard dog inside who was leading around a man with a flat-top haircut. The man's job was to help the dog sniff out suspicious things. I sent my suitcase through the theft detector and emptied my pockets of everything, and they passed the wand over my genitalia, and then the guard said: "Pull your pants legs up, please, so I can see your socks." So I did. They were Thorlos, and they wicked away foot sweat like nobody's tomorrow. Roz gave them to me for Christmas two years ago.

There was Plexiglas an inch thick at the passport office on the second floor. A man in a neat blue State Department blazer asked me some polite questions, and then he clipped my papers together with a comically large paper clip and told me to wait till I heard my number. So I waited. An English mother and her four-year-old girl were there, and the girl had a stuffed baby tiger that, when she squeezed it, meowed. "Did you hear that animal noise?" said a woman. Another woman said: "I think it was the tiger." And the first woman nodded, reassured.

Then my number came up, and a wide man said I would get my passport at three o'clock. So I went up to the sixth floor and bought a tuna sub. The man who sold it to me leaned very close to the keys when he was ringing up my order. His seeing-eye dog sat with very good dog posture behind him on a Polartec blanket. I thanked him and thought the world was an okay place.

Then I went down to the atrium, and I sat and ate the sandwich, looking at a mural of huge blowups of Tip O'Neill smiling with presidents and senators.

After a while I called Roz and told her I was eating a very good submarine sandwich in the Tip O'Neill building and that I'd grown fond of the building and I didn't want to leave it and fly to Switzerland and give a master class on being a poet or be in a panel discussion on the meters of love, because I had nothing to tell them.

"Just tell them why you like poetry," Roz said.

"I'm not at all sure I do like poetry," I said.

"Yes, you do. I know you. You just need some sleep, that's all."

I was quiet for a moment, thinking. "Is Todd being helpful and nice?" I asked. Rather maliciously. Todd was the man whom she'd gone out with a few times. He was an ex–software person who now owned an art gallery in Exeter and wore soft expensive corduroy shirts.

"He's not particularly nice, but he is helpful," she said.

"Oh," I said.

I asked her if I should consider having an affair with a poet in Switzerland, assuming I could find a poet to have an affair with. Trying to be carelessly flirtatious, blowing it.

She sounded surprised. "Do you want to?"

"There would be pain and suffering after," I said. "Probably not. I'm just asking."

Roz hesitated. She said: "I would say—don't."

"Okay," I said. "Thanks for your advice."

"You know of course that I love you," she said.

I SHOWED the airport guards my stiff blue passport and they didn't say, Sir, this document is laughably new—this document didn't even exist a few hours ago. No, they waved me on. I popped into the airport bookstore, which was clean with blond wood going way up to the ceiling. It was the best airport bookstore I'd ever been in, and I liked it so much that I bought John Ashbery's latest book of poems, even though I don't need more books of poetry and can't afford them. Ashbery's photo was on the back, and I saw that he was looking older and even a little bit witchlike now with a downturned mouth. He was born in 1927. He has won every poetry prize known to man or beast, and he was part of that whole ultracool inhuman unreal absurdist fluorescent world of the sixties and seventies in New York. Once he'd edited an art magazine, *Art News*. Even his name is coolly, absurdly, missing one of its Rs.

I knew a little about that art world, or thought I did, in an odd way. One summer when I was fourteen I took care of a cat at a house owned by two gay minimalist painters, Jerry and Sandy. All their walls were flat white, and there were dozens of their paintings up, huge paintings, with silver ovals of metallic paint sprayed from a slight angle, dripping a little bit. The lonely cat roamed this white minimalist house, meowing in a whiskey voice. While she purred beside me, I sat on the minimalist black couch and read copies of *Artforum* and *Art News* from the neat pile on the coffee table. I was hoping to find paintings of naked women, and there weren't as many as you would expect in those magazines because abstraction was confoundedly in vogue. There was an article about a man who cut his palms and the bottoms of his feet with a razor and photographed them healing.

Now I associate people like John Ashbery and Frank O'Hara with this arty cool minimalist house where I catsat. And I'd never really cottoned to Ashbery's *Self-Portrait in a Convex Mirror,* the book that won three awards and made him known throughout the free-verse universe. I'd tried to read it a few times and failed. It's arbitrary. It reads as if it's written by a cleverly programmed random-phrase generator. It doesn't sing.

But Ashbery is old now and therefore more likable. And one of his former students once told me that when Ashbery had a few drinks he got quite silly and giggly and sat on the floor. And the new book had beautiful poem titles in a special typeface, and it had a beautiful cover, and the blurbs were spare and piercing, and although the poems themselves weren't heartbreakers, the book made me think of the sound of someone closing the door of a well-cared-for pale blue Infiniti on a late-summer evening in the gravel overflow parking lot of a beach hotel that had once been painted by Gretchen Dow Simpson.

So I bought the Ashbery and the hell with it.

ROETHKE SAID that a country can really sustain only fifteen poets at a time, which is about right. These are people who are poking and prodding at the language in a very intimate way, and there's only so much of that poking at any one time that the language can endure. And yet in Switzerland there were masses of them. There were poets from Michigan, and poets from San Francisco, and from Miami, and from Iowa, and from Brooklyn, and from some place in Tennessee, and from Amherst, Massachusetts, and from Brattleboro, Vermont. And there were Canadian poets, and a beautiful woman poet from Piombino, which is a town in Italy, who wore pale green gloves. And there were poets from Trinidad, from Ruritania, Bali, Belgium, Austria, the Czech Republic, all over the place. Most of them spoke English. And they were laughing, and they had their name tags on. Everyone was furtively checking everyone's name tag, listening for a bell-tinkle of recognition. They were all being international poets in one place. The noise was incredible. Poets jabbering, poets laughing, a few poets looking hollow-eyed and glum. There was something wonderful seeing them in the room together, but also something a little perverse about it, too, like those kinds of chocolate cake that are filled with inner goops of extra chocolate, that have names like chocolate convulsion, chocolate seizure, chocolate climax. Then suddenly word flew through the room like wildfire—

Paul Muldoon was there! Paul Muldoon! Paul Muldoon! He
was besieged. I ran into him in the hall later near the late-
registration table. There was a lithograph of an alpine scene
behind his head. He said, "Why don't you send me some of
your new work?" I squared my shoulders and said I would,
Paul, thanks.

The gathering was called the Global Word Congress, and
the air was so thin at that altitude that you had to stop every
so often to catch your breath, and it changed the way you
thought after a while. Some of the poets were being paid to
be there. Most of them were paying to be there. We all slept
in the ski lodges.

On the second day was the panel discussion with Renee
Parker Task and two other people on "The Meters of Love."
Renee was brilliant and distant and wise; my enraging blushing tongue-tiedness kicked in early as I knew it would, and
I went all silent and shifty. I made an unnatural snort of a
laugh when Renee mentioned "the pentameter line." Then
I thought, Pull yourself together, you cairn of burning garbage, you're not going to get many more chances like this. So
I talked about scansion and enjambment and the importance
of the invisible rest, and I said that pentameter was really a
waltz, and I talked about how some enjambments made Louise Bogan shudder and rightly so, and then something strange
came over me and I opened my mouth and out of it came
the tune I'd made up for the first stanza of Bogan's "Roman
Fountain."

Afterward a woman from New York came up and asked me what the name was of the poem about the fountain and I told her. She said, " 'Rush to its rest' is really nice," and I nodded, and I thought I'd at least done something good in offering them some Louise Bogan.

THE MASTER CLASS I gave had a rocky moment. I told them to copy poems out, and to start by saying what they actually wanted to say, and to read their drafts aloud in foreign accents, and to clean out their offices, and to make two supporting columns when they packed their books in a box, and I described trying to edit an anthology and how crazy it made me, and I heard myself sounding more or less like a professional poet. Which amazed me.

And then a man of forty or so, with a French accent, asked, "How do you achieve the presence of mind to initiate the writing of a poem?" And something cracked open in me, and I finally stopped hoarding and told them my most useful secret. The only secret that has helped me consistently over all the years that I've written. I said, "Well, I'll tell you how. I ask a simple question. I ask myself: What was the very best moment of your day?" The wonder of it was, I told them, that this one question could lift out from my life exactly what I will want to write a poem about. Something that I hadn't known was important will leap up and hover there in front of me, saying *I* am—*I* am the best moment of the day. I noticed two people were writing down what I was saying. Often, I went on, it's a moment when you're waiting for someone, or you're driving somewhere, or maybe you're just walking diagonally across a parking lot and you're admiring the oil stains and the dribbled tar patterns. One time it was when I was driving past a certain house that was screaming with sunlitness on its white clapboards, and then I plunged through tree shadows that splashed and splayed over the windshield. I thought, Ah, of course—I'd forgotten. You, windshield shadows, you are the best moment of the day. "And that's my secret, such as it is," I said.

They all looked at me, and I looked at them. I was the teacher. I was the authority. And then I said, "Of course, it hasn't worked all that well for me. My first book was okay. But you know what Amy Lowell said. She said, 'Poetry is a young man's job.' " And then I burst into tears.

No wonder they call it bursting. It's a sudden outflipping of the lips and an explosion of liquid from behind the eyelids. Everything that's inside is suddenly coming out. It's really a physical event. You're literally shaking with sobs. Fortunately it didn't last too long.

I apologized and sniffed and smeared my fists in my eyes and collected myself. Then I cleared my throat and I said, more formally, "That's about all I have." The class broke for buffet supper in the Rimbaud Room.

I STARTED UP a path toward one of the mountain cableways. There were hundreds of ideally spaced dandelions on sharply tilting fields, and there was a remote clink of sheep bells, which are similar to cowbells. It seems that sheep farming receives government subsidies in Switzerland so that the clink will continue. And on every path were more wandering poets. You turned a corner and there was another out-of-breath, sweaty, wandering poet. Some had little notebooks, some had cameras, some held a precious paperback. I saw a little red-haired man in a velvet jacket carrying Charles Simic's poems—the edition with the beautifully empty paper bag on it. I said, "Algernon?" He shook his head. I said, "Oh, sorry."

I kept climbing, and then I stopped and sat on a bench and looked across a valley at a distant triangular mountain. The mountain was white, because it was covered with snow, and it looked almost flat—perhaps a trick of the rarefied air. I sat and thought about having a crying jag in my own master class, and then I noticed that the mountain was doing something unusual: it was reflecting quite a lot of white light toward the shadowy mountain that we poets were on. It sent its sideways light deep into the underbranches of the woods, and it made the sedums grow there with unnatural vigor. The sedums were growing in reflected Swiss mountain snowlight. And that was the best moment of the day.

Later a woman told me that when she took LSD she thought she could unscrew her breasts and hand them out to people to use as drinking bowls.

I kept my word to Roz and didn't have an affair, which wasn't too difficult because there was no possibility of it.

17

I WROTE TWENTY-THREE POEMS on the plane back from Switzerland. I always write lots of poems on airplanes, but this was a personal best. When I got home, I saw that Nan's son, Raymond, had piled my mail neatly on the kitchen table. I stared for a long time into my dry beautiful sink. The disposal said "IN-SINK-ERATOR." I'd never read my own disposal before.

Then I sat down at the kitchen table for three days and I put together a clean draft of the introduction to *Only Rhyme* and sent it off to Gene. I wore the same shirt the whole time so as not to lose momentum. The introduction explains things, but clumsily. Everything is much quieter and more filled with exceptions than how I've presented it. But at least there are things I've said that I know are true. I'm happy about that. It's two hundred and thirty pages long.

I called Roz and told her I'd written twenty-three poems and the introduction to *Only Rhyme* and would she move back in with me. She called back and said she didn't want to move back in—that she'd spent a lot of money at IKEA and gotten her place the way she wanted it, so not right now. But did I want to come over for dinner on Saturday? I said yes, I did, I very much did.

I'M WORKING for Victor now, painting houses. Or "Vick," as he likes to be called. Much much better than teaching. Painting houses inside and out, jabbing the brush into corners and clapboard seams. It helps me think. I'm up on an aluminum ladder for real. Being paid for my work. The first evening of Vick's poetry series is going to be devoted to Sara Teasdale. I sent a letter to Mary Oliver inviting her to come up. I doubt she will, but it's fun to invite her.

I wonder what it must be like to be part of something ongoingly huge like a number-one sitcom or part of a magazine when it's in its golden moment—like *The New Yorker* in the thirties—or a fashionable restaurant or a hit musical. Something that everyone wants to think about at the same time. Some people have that privilege. Most don't. And the ones who do are no more content than I am.

Out of the poems I wrote on the plane, I sent three off to this year's *TLS* poetry competition. Alice Quinn and Mick Imlah are the judges. Good old Alice. I know I won't win, but it's like inviting Mary Oliver to our series—a welcome flutter of excitement. And Gene has now read the introduction to *Only Rhyme*. "We're going to need to make some cuts," he said, but he said it'll do. So I'll get a pale green check from him. I've invited Roz to come over to play badminton, also Nan and Chuck and Raymond. I've taught Smacko not to bite the birdie by hitting it out onto the grass and then rewarding him with a crouton when he doesn't lunge.

The summer's over. It's fall. Shadows on the windshield. Rest.

About the Author

NICHOLSON BAKER was born in 1957 and attended the Eastman School of Music and Haverford College. He is the author of several novels, including *The Mezzanine, Vox*, and *The Fermata*, and four works of nonfiction: *U and I, The Size of Thoughts, Double Fold* (winner of the 2002 National Book Critics Circle Award), and *Human Smoke*, which was a *New York Times* and *Los Angeles Times* bestseller. He lives in Maine.